D0524511

Gene Kemp grew up near Tamworth in the Midlands. She took a degree at Exeter University, taught, married and had three children. She is best known for her Cricklepit School stories, which include *The Turbulent Term of Tyke Tiler* (a winner of the Carnegie Medal and the Children's Rights Award), *Gowie Corby Plays Chicken, Charlie Lewis Plays for Time* (runner-up for the Whitbread Award in 1985), and *Just Ferret*, which was a runner-up for the Smarties Award in 1990. In addition, she has written *The Clock Tower Ghost, Jason Bodger and the Priory Ghost* (short stories) and a poetry anthology. She also writes for TV and radio. In 1984 she was awarded an honorary degree for her books, which are translated into numerous languages.

GENE KEMP

Snaggletooth's Mystery
or, The Alternative Cricklepit Story

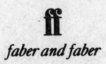

faber and faber

First published in 2002
by Faber and Faber Limited
3 Queen Square London WC1N 3AU

Photoset by RefineCatch Ltd, Bungay, Suffolk
Printed in England by Mackays of Chatham plc

A CIP record for this book
is available from the British Library

ISBN 0–571–21045–7

2 4 6 8 10 9 7 5 3 1

For Suzy
with love and thanks

What did one ghost say to another ghost?

I don't know. What did one ghost say to another ghost?

Do you believe in people?

People in the Book

―――――

At School

Mrs Alicia Markham, M.Ed., PhD, Head Teacher
Mr William Merchant, BA, MA, Deputy Head
Mr Norman Warpole, B.Ed.
Miss Sylvia Beattie, B.Ed.
Mr Armstrong, PE Teacher
Miss Penelope Farthing, Classroom Assistant
Mr Giles Figgis, School Secretary
Mrs Violet Jefferson-Smythe, Caretaker
Cyril Jefferson-Smythe, Husband
Mrs Cynthia Somers, JP, Chair of School Governors

Class 6W

Snaggletooth Watson	Lucy Chinn
Ryan Tiler	Sally Fox
Shahid Malik	Tasha Santini
Strawberry Rainbird	Lulu Sercombe
Rod Stringer	Santia Bliss
Matthew Ernest	Boris Ladislaw

Class 6P
Barry Morse

Ghosts?
Grandad
Two children
St Sativola

Family
Dad – Bryan Watson
Mum – Cecilia Morgan
Romilly Watson
Miranda (Mizza)
  Watson

Cassandra (Cass)
  Watson
Cameron Morgan
Kris Morgan
(Snaggletooth) Watson
Tegwyn (Teggy) Watson

Friend
Mariella Higgins

Boris's Family
Grandma Ladislaw
Persephone Ladislaw

It was a bit of a giggle really. We were bored one wet Sunday afternoon – you know the feeling: time lasts forever and you don't know what to do that you haven't already done. We were round at our house, Strawberry, Shahid and me, and everybody kept saying, 'Go away,' 'Scram,' 'Push off,' 'Get lost,' 'You're redundant,' so at last, we ended up messing about with Dad's super computer which we're not supposed to touch, but he wasn't there that Sunday, was he?

It was Shahid who thought of it, but I ended up as editor. Shahid said he didn't want it and Strawberry said she was no good at telling people what to do so it had to be me.

Anyway, we knocked up a few posters and asked for news. We argued for ages about the title – the *Cricklepit Echo*, the *Gazette*, the *Cricklepit Knowall*, the *Times*, the *Thunderer*, the *Truth Teller*, the *Cricklepit*

Gossip – and ended up with *Chronicle* because of the two Cs. Then we argued about what to put in it.

At last we stuck up the posters, news came rushing in and we did our first *Chronicle*. This was in the autumn term just before Christmas and everyone took to reading it – the *Chronicle* was a Success!

So we kept it going. There's always some news – match results, a chickenpox epidemic, Mr Snelling, a supply teacher, running off with one of the dinner ladies, Mrs Purling, and the thousand and million things that happen in school. A cure for nit infestation sold dozens – we were charging 2p a newspaper by then. We needed funds as Dad made us help pay towards computer costs.

And so it went on, and I got the writing bug, thinking up articles, always writing, surfing, writing, printing, writing, while school life was going on all around us.

'I want to be a journalist,' I told Sir, Mr Merchant. He's written a book or two himself. History. So you can say something like that to him without being told to try hard with your spelling. He took it seriously.

'Remember, journalists should always tell the truth. Sometimes, just to sell more papers, they print lies or things that shouldn't be published. But telling the truth is a journalist's job.'

'Of course we'll always tell the truth in the *Chronicle*!'

So the *Chronicle* was born.

And then, then in the summer term – A SCOOP! A SCOOP OF SCOOPS!

Here goes. Oh, about the truth. Well, we tried. But it was harder than we thought.

THE CRICKLEPIT CHRONICLE

THE EYES – THE EARS – THE VOICE – OF THE SCHOOL

News / Adverts / Stories / Jokes / Pictures / Recipes / Cartoons / Fashion / Gossip (Who's going out with who?) / The Internet / And much, much more!

Editor	*Assistant Editor*	*Reporter*
Snaggletooth Watson	Shahid Malik	Strawberry Rainbird

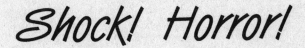

A brand new purple car belonging to Mrs Somers, Chair of Governors, was vandalised yesterday afternoon. The car was parked at the front of the school. Rear lights, bumper and the back windows were smashed.

Police were called and questioned teachers and pupils, but no one said anything at the time except the school secretary who reported seeing two black raggedy figures flitting past, but this was discounted.

<u>Later</u> – after further questioning by Mrs Somers a witness was found, following which a top-year boy was excluded.

One

─────────

My kid sister (the littlest one, Teggy – I've got three more, which shouldn't happen to a saint, let alone me) was sitting plonk in the middle of the stairs that morning, taking up all the room with her teddies and talking to Grandad. OK by me, except he died last year. He used to live with us. She talks to him every day. Only one who listens to her, she says.

'Move, fleabag!' I yell. 'I need my bag and it's in the bedroom. We've got SATs today.'

'Get stuffed,' she shrieks. But she moves and shoots downstairs fast so I can get to my room. No school-bag there.

'Who's got my bag?' I bellow down into the hall, now full of nutters surging round and round, up and down, scrabbling for things, with Mizza singing her rotten solo for her school concert. Again. Mum's shouting and our dog Boxie's howling 'cos he knows it's school and he'll be left behind. You'd've thought he'd be grateful. I rush down to the kitchen. I gotta have that bag. People who forget homework are slaughtered dead.

'Get out of my way,' I yell at the cat lying on top of the hamster cage with his 'I'll get you one of these days' look on his whiskery ginger face. He spits at me and hisses, which is a bit unfair.

'Which one of you lot's had my bag?'

Nobody moves, surprise, surprise. They're all too busy screeching.

'Where's my anorak?'

'Who's taken my bag?'

'Have you done my packed lunch? You know it's our school trip today,' Kris yells.

Above all this rises the sound of Mum and it's not the sound of music.

'Shut up, all of you! Why can't you look after your own things? Who do you think I am? An octopus? Teggy, put on your shoes! Mizza, where have you got to? Get ready NOW!'

Dad shoots out of his room where he's been hiding away from it all.

'Shut up, you lot! Can't we ever get any peace in this house?'

Dad's always asking for peace, but not getting it. And he certainly isn't now, as a Barbie doll drops on to his bald head over the banisters, followed by Mizza's demon laugh. He yells loudly, then goes back in his room, rubbing his head and muttering.

'Grandad says look under the stairs,' shouts Teggy, popping up under my nose, like a jack-in-the-box. 'Your bag'll be there.'

It is, and I slam out of the house before I have to walk to school with any of them. And there just coming out of his house is my mate Shahid, with his mother shouting after him. So's mine. After me, I mean.

'You got your homework?' they both call.

'Yeah.'

'Good luck with SATs!'

'Yuck!'

Two

We're finally here. The thing the teachers have been preparing us for all year has arrived. It's the moment of truth, the deciding factor, the score to settle all scores . . . for Pete's sake, it's only a test!

Who cares how clever you are? And why do you need a test to tell you how clever you are? From the way my friends were acting you'd think it was the divider between heaven and hell, or something!

At last we're seated neatly in our desks, arranged in pairs, places labelled, pens poised, brains at the ready.

'You may begin,' Mr Warpole's voice booms above the nervous silence.

Have you ever noticed how silence can be louder than noise? Well, that's how it is now with twenty-seven kids, terrified and clammy, being forced to do a test. Why? Must be a law somewhere in the clouds. ALL CHILDREN MUST SUFFER SATS.

The silence flattens us like a smother blanket. The

only sound's a *brr brr* of a pneumatic drill in the distance.

Oops! Back to the test. Useless sitting there listening to far-off pneumatic drills. Daydreaming (again). Got to get going. I glance round the room to help me on my way. What are the rest up to?

Matthew Ernest drops his pen, making a loud noise as it hits the floor. Mr Warpole looks up and silences the wretched pen with his steely stare. Poor Matthew turns beetroot-red and sinks to the floor to pick it up. He's OK, but a bit creepy. Tries hard is written all over his forehead.

My mate Shahid's writing away like his fingers got the itches. But then he always does. Writes faster, more words per minute than anyone in the school. Except me.

I look at the clock. How much longer have we got? Better fill in some questions quickly. Then back to people-watching (much more fun). Strawberry catches my eye and swivels hers.

There's Lucy Chinn, gnawing at her pencil, her snobby face concentrated in a horrid stare, her ears sticking out a mile as she pushes her hair back – hang on, she's got jug ears. I've not noticed before. So she's *not* perfect, then, she's got jug ears! This calls for further investigation! An article in the *Cricklepit Chronicle* – 'Year 6: Jug Ears and their Owners'?

A few more questions first. Then I see Sally Fox's sweating face – hang on, again, is she crying? She would. What a load of fuss over nothing. I mean, what's the big deal? (Yeah, it's easy for you, Snaggle, your parents won't create merry hell if you don't get twenty starred Level Fives. But still.)

Sally's surrounded. Lucky shoelaces, lucky charms, a silver locket, two handkerchiefs, four pencils, three pens, felt tips and a photo of her family! I'm surprised she doesn't drown in all that stuff. I feel quite sorry for her, really, how awful it must be to let a few measly tests run your life.

Some more questions – quickly, finish 'em off. Then you can people-watch. More copy for the magazine. Hey! What's that?

The new kid, who only came yesterday afternoon, has buried his head on his arms on his paper. And his shoulders are shaking – poor thing. Fancy making him do SATs on almost his first day! Oh, help! He really is crying. Isn't ole Warpole going to do something about it? Ole Warpole is bent over his papers, and no! he looks as if he's falling asleep. What cheek! I know he was a hundred and ninety last birthday, but he's got thousands (well, twenty-seven, no, it must be twenty-eight with the new one) of kids here in a state of nervous desperation to please their families, and he's dropping off!

'Mr Warpole,' I call out.

'Be quiet! You're doing a test. Remember?'

'But Sir, the new boy is crying. Look!'

He looks and comes over to the new boy, whose face is streaky with dirt and tears.

'What's the matter, boy? You knew it was the SATs tests today, didn't you?'

More sobs and tears. The kid's trying to bury himself in the question paper. I want to go to him and say, 'Kid, it doesn't matter, honest. Don't worry. I'll do it for you.'

People are turning round and staring. The test's coming to a dead halt. Anything for a change.

'What is it, boy? I can't help you if you don't tell me.'

More sobs. Can anything ever be worth all this awful sorrow?

'Just write your name. Boris, isn't it?'

'I-I-I can't.'

'What d'you mean, you *can* write your name, can't you?'

'No-no-no.'

He tries to burrow right down into the desk.

'Get on with the test, the rest of you!' roars ole' Warpole, glaring. He swings round the class.

'You!'

'Yes, Sir,' I answer, wondering what I've done wrong now.

'You've finished, haven't you? You're always quick, aren't you?'

Makes it sound like a crime.

'Yessir.'

'Well, go and get Miss Farthing, the classroom assistant. She's supposed to be here anyway. And hurry!'

'Yessir.'

So there I am scurrying through the school mad-ferret fashion, and at last I find Miss Farthing, classroom assistant, in the sick room, bathing a first year busily bleeding all over the place.

'Come! Come on, Penny, it's an emergency.'

'So's this. Look at him!' The kid wails loudly. 'Anyway, this school's one long emergency. So what's new?'

'Come ON! Mr Warpole said "Hurry"!'

'Right. We'll all come. Billy, hold this cotton wool to your head. Look after him, Snaggle.'

Back in the classroom once more, Mr Warpole takes Boris out into the corridor, Miss Farthing sits with the test-takers, and I am left holding cotton wool to Billy's bleeding head, while the others SAT on.

Ten minutes left, the clock on the pale pink wall says. This is utterly boring! Think of what I could be doing – reading a book, playing on the Playstation, practising my violin, learning my new part in the play, doing a workout, cleaning out the gerbils (all thirty of them), collecting copy for the *Cricklepit Chronicle*. Yet here we are, sitting SAT-ting, one kid outside crying, another inside bleeding. But then, of course, school is there to make you miserable.

The bell rings! Yes! Time's up! Now, have we got to go over the test to see the million and one things we've got wrong? Hope not, boring, boring. Where's ole Warpole? What happens now?

Ole Warpole comes hurrying back in, takes Billy off me and off Billy toddles with Miss Farthing holding his hand. Sweet. Which is more than ole' Warpole is. He gathers in the papers.

'Please, where's the new boy gone, Sir?' asks Lucy Chinn. It would be. I look to see her jug ears, but her yellow hair's covered them up again. He doesn't answer.

'Fancy not being able to WRITE your own NAME,' she mutters to Sally.

'Fancy! Tut tut, squeak, squeak, giggle, giggle.'

'You can go now. Quietly,' says ole Warpole.

'Headache, Sir?' asks Strawberry.

'Be quiet. Just open the door!'

'I can't, Sir.'

'What do you mean, you can't?'

'It's stuck, Sir.'

'Of course it isn't stuck. Let me do it!'

The door stays shut.

'I just don't believe it!' Ole Warpole grits his teeth, or what was left of them (like the old boy on telly). He looks terrible. We all jostle round him. Test over – we want out of here.

Everyone's having a go. Everyone's sure *they're* the one, the one with the special power. So why isn't it opening? It was OK when I fetched Penny Farthing and when ole Warpole took the new kid wherever he'd taken him.

'Where's the key?'

No key.

'Anyone got a bit of wire? My Dad can open anything with a bit of bent wire,' Rod Stringer says proudly, making us laugh. Rod's a joker. He opens a cupboard and fishes out an old coathanger. Very handy.

Mr Warpole isn't Rod's dad, surprise, surprise, and he still can't open the door, especially with a bent wire coathanger.

'Come on, let's push. Together now!'

The classroom door opens on to a short flight of stairs, our school being funny like that. It's an old fossil of a school curling round and round on itself. Ole Warpole pushes, Matthew pushes, we all push – all together now! And at last the door flies open. So do we. Fly, I mean.

Flying, falling. Guess who's at the bottom of the heap. Poor, poor Mr Warpole.

We pick ourselves up. But poor Mr Warpole still lies there, groaning, flat out, not looking good. He lifts his head as we lift him. A bump is rising, like in Tom and Jerry. Poor ole Warpole.

Far away the pneumatic drill roars, *brr brr brr*.

Three

Same day, later, lunchtime.

Chewing my last bit of gum, pushing it behind and around my snaggletooth, thinking up some more articles for the *Cricklepit Chronicle*, I wander out of the playground and on to the field. Behind me wild yells are going up.

'Ryan's back! He's come! Ryan's come! Ryan! Ryan!'

What, in the afternoon? Funny time to turn up. This needs investigation. Definitely. So it's the return of Ryan, School Hero and School Villain – yeah, he's both of 'em, both at once. I turn to go and join the crowd, then stop, for in front of me is the Girl Gang – Lucy Chinn and her lot, Tasha, Lulu, Sally Fox and Santia – dancing, jigging, hair swinging like the TV ads, round a kid hunched back against the wall, the new kid who cried, and who's been looking miserable ever since.

No, he's not looking miserable now – he's looking terrified.

'What's your name?'

'Why d'you wear those clothes?'

'They're disgusting.'

'Where did you go after the test?'

'Tell us. Tell us. Tell, tell, tell.'

'Are you poor?'

'You look poor.'

'Is it true you can't read? Or write your own name?'

'His name's Boris!' cries Tasha.

'Boris Popinovski!' Giggle, giggle, nudge, nudge, hair flinging, fling, fling.

'That's why he can't write his own name!'

'FANCY NOT BEING ABLE TO WRITE YOUR OWN NAME!'

More dancing and cartwheels.

'Poor, poor 'ickle Boris! Never mind, we'll take care of you! Boggy Boris!'

Really into it now, whirling and twirling round him, long blonde tatty hair, ginger curls, black rasta with beads, long mouse and streaky yellow, all the TV ads there ever were. Stuck against the wall he can't get away. He tries to curl up even smaller. Santia is turning cartwheels like a firework going off. Good thing trousers are our school uniform or we'd get an eyeful. Lucy stops swirling and flinging her hair around and spots me.

'Push off, Snaggle!'

Behind me in the playground I can hear shouts of 'Ryan' fighting it out with the row of the pneumatic drills. Ryan, Ryan, Ryan, *brr, brr, brr*, Ryan's back. Rah, rah, rah, Ryan, roars Ryan's fan club.

'Don't worry. I'm off!' I shout, but the kid's trying to struggle out of the semicircle round him.

'Wait for me! Wait! Snaggle!' he croaks and that gets me. He's remembered me from the test.

'You should be in school uniform, Boris Horace. We wear uniform here.'

'You'll get into awful trouble, bullying,' I yell. 'It's not on.'

'We're not bullying – and you wouldn't tell anyway, would you, Snaggle, toothy, woothy . . . ?'

'I might write it up in the *Chronicle* so LET HIM GO!'

'Get your own life, Snaggle. Instead of writing about ours!'

And they burst forth into one of their awful songs. Tasha writes them and Lucy and Sally and the others sing and play them.

> *We're the Girl Gang*
> *Leaders of the pack*
> *Tall and slim and beautiful*
> *Get a load of that!*

I step forward to grab the kid and get pushed back.

Then the cry from the playground round the corner goes up, really loud this time.

'Ryan's back. Ryan's back at school. RYAN! RYAN!'

Our boy Ryan's getting the star treatment. There'll be trouble.

The Girl Gang stop as if their batteries have been switched off.

'Let's go see. Come on,' yells Lucy.

And they're gone, flying feet in snazzy pricey trainers, swinging hair, speeding round the corner in a shower of shrieks: 'Ryan, Ryan!'

The kid shakes himself like a furry animal and manages a grin.

'Thanks. For stopping *them*, I mean.'

'S'OK. But it wasn't me, really. It was Ryan. Come on.'

We turn round the corner into the playground heaving with kids.

'Who's he?'

'A kid in my class. Our class. School's Number One Super Hero. He's been away and now he's back. That's all.'

'Was he ill?'

'No. He was excluded.'

'What's that?'

'Shut out of school.'

'Why? I thought they *made* you go to school. They

15

made me. I wish they'd exclude me. I don't want to be here.'

'You get excluded if you're wicked.'

'Is Ryan wicked?'

'Nah. But some people think so.'

'Teachers?'

'Governors, mostly, I think. But come on. If you want to see him we'll have to get a move on. Oh, there's the whistle. We'll have to go in now, Boris. This way. Just follow me.'

Brr brr.

'What's the noise?'

'They're digging up the drains round here.'

'Sounds like they're letting all sort of things out.'

'What things?'

'I dunno. Ghosts. Old things. Maybe.'

'You're crazy, kid.'

Four

Mr Merchant, Sir, Deputy Head, Second in Command(!), sits in the teacher's desk – we sit silently in ours. No sign of Ryan. Sir looks stern.

'Mr Warpole has had to go home. He's had a very nasty knock on the head and he may be concussed. He may have to have some sick leave. Until we can get a supply teacher, I shall be taking you.'

Sally Fox starts to say, 'Goody, goody,' and then stops. Sir's not looking at all 'Goody, goody,' more like Demon Sir, with the power of life or death. We quiver a bit, because he's not ole Warpole. He's tough. Ole Warpole was quite sweet, really. He used to have those yellow smiley faces stuck up outside his door, 'Be Happy,' although they never looked right for him. But he could be an old softy at times. We were a bit much for him, I think. And he was old and wrinkly.

'We did our SATs this morning,' put in Lucy Chinn, batting her eyelashes and whooshing her hair at Sir (like the TV ads). 'It would be nice to do something nice this afternoon, Sir. Please.'

Sir answers:

'I've always hated that word "nice",

Especially when you use it twice.'

Is he joking, making funny rhymes? He's in a weird mood. Has he flipped at last? Ole Warpole has. Is Sir going the same way? (NB. Investigate mental health of staff?)

' "Nice" originally meant "exact", Lucy, so try using another word next time. And no, we're actually going to work this afternoon. Don't bother groaning. I might add an extra five minutes for each groan.'

'Why are you in a mood, Sir?' asks Strawberry. He likes Strawberry. Everyone likes Strawberry. Except Lucy Chinn, who only likes Lucy Chinn.

'I'm worried about Mr Warpole. And I'm losing all my free periods that I use to keep this school from falling to pieces, which is quite difficult, strangely enough.'

'Where's Ryan? Is he coming back into our class, Sir?'

'Perhaps. Now let's get on, shall we?' He waits. We wait. And wait.

'Cholera,' he announces slowly, at last.

Oh, he's really flipped now. What's cholera when it's

at home? What's cholera to do with anything? And what's it to do with us? And what is it anyway?

He answers almost immediately.

'The most dreaded of the diseases was cholera, the unpredictable scourge of the new urban England, the Angel of Death with terror under the shadow of its wings.'

We aren't fidgeting. Something in his voice and the words he uses holds us still. I look at Strawberry and she looks at me. A shadow falls across the classroom. But it's only a cloud going over the sun. And it's only Sir speaking. Surely.

'Listen. It's 1832. We're just before the old Victorian times we hear a lot about and which you've done quite a lot of work on. Outside the sun shines. It's July, hot sunshine. Lovely summer. Someone, quite well up till then, feels giddy, sick. Cramps begin at the top of the fingers and toes and spread all over the body. Vomiting and diarrhoea start . . . '

'Oh, no,' moans Sally. He picks up a book, opens it at a bookmarked page and reads . . .

' . . . features become sharp, the eyes sink in and the face becomes terrified and wild. Lips, face, neck, hands, feet, arms and thighs turn blue, or purple-black. The fingers and toes go small, the skin wrinkles, the nails become pearly. The skin is deadly cold and flabby, the veins black, the tongue is white, breathing is fast and uneven. The patient speaks in a whisper, struggles for breath and points to his heart.'

'Sir, please stop. Don't do this to us. My mum wouldn't like it,' wails Sally.

'What could you do to stop it? To cure it?' asks Shahid Malik.

'Antibiotics, plenty of water and drinks, warmth. But . . . they didn't have antibiotics in 1832. They were first used much later, in the Second World War. And the water – now that's a history of its own . . . look up "water" on the Internet for me.'

'Sir, there's always been water . . . '

'Has there? Where's the water in the desert? In a burning forest fire? Where was the water here in 1832?'

'My dad goes mental over the water rates,' put in Rod.

'But what's water got to do with cholera?' asks Shahid.

'That's the million-dollar question that you're finding out the answer to. And now we'll take a break while – you, Snaggle, you're the quickest, fetch me the old map on top of the filing cabinet in the stockroom upstairs. The rest of you can make a get-well-soon card for Mr Warpole, while Boris and I have a chat.'

Five

I stroll along the corridor, stretching time out – even if I am supposed to be the quickest – before I have to get back to the classroom, then up the stairs, with the bend in the middle, that go up to the teachers' old staffroom, the broom cupboard, the stock cupboard and the teachers' cloakroom. This is the spooky bit that scares some kids, for this part of the school is really antique. The old staffroom is always kept locked and the teachers, they say, will only go in there two or three at a time, ever since Mrs Venables found herself shut in for about three hours before her shouting was heard and she was let out. She left. After a bit it was opened again refurbished and made over. Strawberry told us the vicar came and said a prayer there – I'd got measles then, so I couldn't keep an eye on things for the *Chronicle* and Strawberry and Shahid covered for me. Afterwards the staffroom was used again. But no one goes in on their own.

In the stockroom I get the map from the top of the filing cabinet, and suddenly there's Violet, our caretaker, red in the face and puffing loudly as she tries out one key after another in the teachers' cloakroom. Her hair shines a beautiful purple in the gloom. She must've just had it touched up. (Query: what came first? Violet's name or the colour of her hair?)

When she sees me she cries, 'Snaggle, see if you can turn this key. I 'ad a go and couldn't shift it one bit. Then I tried to pull it out and I couldn't.'

She takes an enormous breath and this time pulls the key out of the lock. But the door's still stuck when we try to open it. She holds out the large bunch of keys in her hand.

'Look, I've tried 'em all,' she exclaims. 'No joy. That door won't budge an inch. I think it's locked on the inside. And bolted.'

She bangs on the door. No answer.

'Suppose someone's died in there. Had a heart attack on the seat and puff – gone like that,' I say.

'That's what scares me. Are you OK in there?' she bellows.

Only silence. Not a pleasant silence. A sort of thick, blankety silence, louder than noise.

'I can't hear a thing. Snaggle, put *your* ear to the keyhole and listen.'

I shove my ear to the keyhole, listening, listening.

'Are you OK in there?' I shout. I mean, either they are or they aren't. I can see the headline in the *Chronicle*. 'POPULAR TEACHER found dead in Cricklepit cloakroom.' (Query: which teacher? Which is the one that I wouldn't mind being finished off?)

A faint ringing, far, far away, bringing echoes of – oh, I dunno – something, something old, far away, but here, something earthy that I don't much like. Spooky.

'Let's bash it down!' I suggested.

'Don't be daft. I'd 'ave to pay it back out of wages. It's in the contract. Any damages to be paid for, it says.'

'Is there a small window in there? Then we can get a ladder and climb in from the outside.'

'Yeah. But it's only ever so tiny. I'm a bit too big.' (Violet's small for a hippo, but big for a person.) 'I know. You'll 'ave to do it, Snags. You're skinny enough. I'll hold the ladder. You climb in, go inside, then step over the body if there is one and open the door from the inside. Take the keys with you.'

'What about the ladder?'

'I'd better ask the Head Teacher. Or else I shall 'ave to pay for damages to you or the window. You tell your teacher what you're doing, helping me, and I'll go and ask the Head Teacher if we can use the ladder.'

'Violet, let's do it ourselves. They'll stop us if we ask them.'

'OK.' She grins and nods.

Six

The big storeroom's *under* the school and there you can find everything you can imagine. Shahid says he once saw a coffin, and I know there's some sandstone blocks that Sir says came from the old city walls built by the Romans yonks ago. In this school there are secret hiding places everywhere, 'cos it's like a maze or a snail shell or a fossil that goes round and round into itself, hideaway places you've never even dreamt of. Often the quickest way to get from one place to another is to go right round the outside of the school and pop in the door you want, that is if it's open, 'cos it might be locked these days against some maniac coming in to splatter all us kids with a Kalashnikov, da-da-de-de-da-dit-di-di-splat-deaded. I know the code number for opening the doors, but I don't tell anyone except Strawberry and Shahid. Rod knows, he would. And Ryan. Come to think of it, who doesn't? (Query: school secrets – does everybody know them?)

I follow Violet into the storeroom with rubber PE mats draped over everything. We soon spot a ladder and haul it out towards the playground. The map's still under my arm.

'Hold the other end,' snapped Violet, 'and mind what you're doing. *That* was my big toe!'

We get the ladder out OK, just as some First School kids come toddling past with their teacher. The last one sticks out its tongue and waggles its fingers on its nose at me and whispers, 'Nasty pig,' but I take no notice, though I know it's that horrible little girl, Mariella Higgins, who sometimes comes to tea with my sister and they have little chats with Grandad. I don't care if she does pull faces. I'm happy outside with Violet and a ladder and the 'Investigation of Who or What is Locked in the Teachers' Cloakroom'. (Query: will it do for next week's *Chronicle*? YES! YES! YES!)

'Is that the window?' I ask.

A very small window, four panes only, peeps out from behind a chimney, built in the Middle Ages from the look of it, and just about to fall down in the twenty-first century.

'Could be,' Violet nods.

So we stand up the ladder and Violet manoeuvres it so that the ladder comes just below the flea-sized window.

Seeing how high up it all is, I'm not at all sure that this is a good idea. Maybe it'd be better to get back to the classroom and Sir making get-well cards for ole Warpole. Maybe ladders aren't my thing.

'P'raps we ought to get somebody. To break the door down instead, y'know, Violet.'

'Scared?'

I think of the *Chronicle*. Journalists must be ready to do ANYTHING.

'Nah. Course not.'

I step on to the ladder.

'Violet! Hold it steady now! Don't let go!'

I climb higher, feeling braver. Not much further. Nearly there. This is easy-peasy stuff.

'Should that child really be up there?' screeches a voice like my kid sister blowing a wrong note on her trumpet. I know that voice. Mrs Somers, the Chair of the Governors, JP, has arrived. She's built like a tank with yellow curls. She and Violet together look like a make-over programme: 'Create More Colour In Your Life'.

They say she used to teach here, but couldn't bear to stop bossing people around when she retired, so she got herself made a Governor. And now she's the Chief Chair of the Governors, or whatever it's called, and lots of other things as well. It makes me very depressed to hear her voice, partly because her voice is horrible and I hate her, but also because it means *she* can't be the one dead in the cloakroom. But Violet answers her:

'Special emergency, Mrs Somers. Trouble in the cloakroom and I can't get in, so I've sent Snaggle up there, skinny enough to climb in through that little window, you see. Will you help to hold the ladder as well, Mrs Somers, if you don't mind me asking?'

A moment later there's another voice.

'Mrs Somers, Violet, a pupil – and a ladder. Now enlighten me, please, someone, just what is going on here?'

The clear voice of Mrs Markham, the new Head, rings through the playground and up the ladder to me, where I'm trying to get the window open.

'I need a knife,' I yell down. 'It's a bit stuck up with paint.'

'You two hold the ladder,' cries Violet, 'and I'll take me Stanley knife up.'

'No, no, you'll break the ladder' – Mrs Somers and Mrs Markham together.

'Please hurry. I don't feel safe!'

Feet – not Violet's – come up behind me. Holding tight, I look round to see Mr Merchant, Sir, right behind me. That does it. Everything, the ladder, the sky, me, wobbles.

'Steady there,' says Violet.

'Take care,' cries Mrs Markham, Head Teacher.

'LOOK OUT!' bellows Mrs Somers, Chair.

Sir steadies the ladder and me, gets a knife from his pocket, and loosens the window from behind me. Somehow he pulls the window open. It hits my face and I nearly fall off again. What am I doing here? I must be crazy. I wish I'd never climbed this stinking ladder.

'Ow! Oh! Ah! Look out!' come cries from below.

'Don't mess about. Get in there!'

Sir pushes me through a space the size of a large beetle and I fall sprawling on the floor inside, ouch!

'I'm too big to follow,' he shouts. 'Do you know what to do?'

'Yeah, I think so.' I get up off the floor, feeling weird.

'I'll climb down and come up to you the normal way and hope to meet you. Oh, I'll get the map on the way. You dropped it.' He sounds cross.

'Sir, Sir. Don't blame me. There might be a dead teacher in there and I've got to get it out.'

'Even teachers don't deserve a fate like that. Found dead in school loo. See you in a minute, Snaggle.'

Half the school seems to be down below from the racket I can hear. Then everything's quiet. Very quiet. Thick, fat quiet that I don't like.

I look round. I'm in a narrow passage. I turn just round

a corner and it widens into a large space, full of buckets and mops and squeezy bottles of cleaning stuff. Ahead of me is a door marked 'Ladies'.

I stand still. I'm all alone, I think. Don't like it. But I don't really believe in spooks (or do I?) So I stick out my tongue at whatever isn't there. Yahoo to you, ghosties, pooh, pooh! You don't scare *moi*.

Feel spooked. Ouch, somebody pinching me! Let me out of here! I'm scared. Mr Merchant, don't leave me alone with whatever's here!

RUBBISH! You're OK! AREN'T YOU, SNAGGLE? There's no one here. Remember, reporters must be brave. Think of Kate Adie going everywhere in the world. She's not scared. Is she? (No, but I am.)

I shiver, then push open the door that isn't locked from this side.

I'm in a small cloakroom with washbasins. I push open another door. An icy gust of air blasts round and past me. There's a ringing in my ears. Help! Help!

'Hey,' yells Sir from outside. 'Look out! Ouch! Don't do that!'

'What?'

'Something nearly knocked me off!'

I open the cubicle doors. It's so strange to be in the teachers' loos. They're SACRED!!! Aren't they? (Sacred? Scared? Anagram! Remember for *Chronicle*.)

29

There's no one there. No corpse. No dead teacher. Not even a dead mole.

Oh! Good. Thank goodness. (Oh! Blow. No story in an empty toilet, is there? Don't let anyone know I'm a bit disappointed. What a story it could have been!)

Outside I can hear the pneumatic drills and a ringing noise. Different, all around me and peculiar, making me dizzy, dizzy, dizzy, carrying me far away. Am I going to faint? No, no, no, not me. Not Snaggle.

Then the noise and the ringing are gone. I'm OK, I think. I take the keys Violet gave me and pick out the right one. The door opens easily.

Then I slide the bolt across and run downstairs.

I hand over the keys to Violet.

'Empty?' they all ask, gathering round me. I'm panting, sweating, like I've been running the hundred metres.

'Empty!'

The pneumatic drills roar louder and louder, all round the school.

Seven

I'm congratulated and told off, both at the same time. For climbing a ladder and for climbing a ladder. They say I'm brave and helpful. They say I'm silly and disobedient.

And I mustn't ever stay out of class and climb a ladder ever, ever again. Never ever ever.

And I think that's that.

But next day Violet and me stand in front of Mrs Somers and the governors. Sir's there as well.

'This is a very serious matter,' she announces. 'This child should not have been climbing up a ladder IN school hours and ON the SCHOOL PREMISES. And before I or rather we begin I want to be sure that none of this is reported in the SCHOOL NEWS-PAPER which just lately has BEGUN TO GO TOO FAR!'

She glares at me.

'Don't pull that face, child. Just remember that you must ASK PERMISSION before you write anything or go climbing ladders. Listen to me, EVERYBODY!'

They can't help listening. She sounds like a heavy-metal rock band. Old Mr Setter takes out his hearing aid so he can't hear.

'If this NAUGHTY child had been killed, WE, the governors, would have been held responsible and made to PAY COMPENSATION. Money! A large sum of MONEY!!!'

Didn't know I was worth a large sum of money. Interesting. (NB. Snaggletooth is worth a large sum of MONEY. Dead.)

'Do you understand, child?'

'Yes, but it wouldn't matter to me if I was dead, would it?'

Mrs Somers' face is the same colour as Violet's hair. But Violet's getting ratty too.

'But *you* were there as well. And the Head Teacher. Where is she? And Mr Merchant. It wasn't just me and Snaggle!'

'Quite, Violet, but . . . '

'Don't you Violet me. My name is Mrs Jefferson-Smythe if you don't mind. I'm not Violet to everybody. So there!'

Mr Merchant coughs gently.

'The Head Teacher isn't here because she's showing

a group of other Head Teachers and Inspectors round the school. And the locks of all doors are going to be checked. The locksmith is coming tomorrow so perhaps we may conclude this meeting.'

The governors start to move to the door.

'Just a minute,' shouts Violet. 'I want a word. I been caretaker here for years and no trouble till now. Snaggle and me, we was only trying to help because we thought someone might've passed out in the toilet so I don't appreciate being hauled up here like a criminal. So you can find somebody else to do your cleaning. I'm off!'

And Violet swept out of the door.

'That's all we need,' sighs Mr Merchant. 'It's not easy to find a good caretaker, and Violet has been hard-working, loyal and knows every child in the school.'

'The meeting is closed,' shouts Mrs Somers, and everyone tries to get away as soon as possible just as . . . the school secretary, Mr Figgis, rushes up . . .

'Listen! Come! Come!'

'What's the matter?' asks Mr Merchant.

'Follow me,' cries Mr Figgis, and everyone goes after him to the flight of stairs leading to the you-know-spooky old staffroom, with me tagging along behind them to see what's going on. What's going on are shouts and banging and stamping, like an elephant's war dance – not that I've ever heard one, but you get the idea. Some of the shouts sound foreign.

Mr Figgis stops outside the door and tries to open it while the rest of us stand still.

'We'll soon get you out of there!' shouts Mr Merchant through the keyhole.

'It's the same thing happening all over again. They can't open the door,' says Mr Figgis. 'I think we'll have to break it down.'

He tries to shove his shoulders against the door like in the films. The door doesn't budge, but at least they've gone quiet inside.

'Let me climb the ladder again and get in through the window,' I say hopefully.

'Oh, no, not all that again,' says Mr Merchant, and his face looks a bit as if he's trying not to laugh, but he manages easily once Mrs Somers tells him what to do – he just looks fed up instead.

In the end they fetch Violet's husband, who's so big he makes Violet look tiny, and he breaks the door down, releasing Head Teachers, Inspectors etc., and the school cat if we'd got one. (Query: why haven't we got a school cat?)

I go back to the classroom, head buzzing and

whizzing with IDEAS and weird thoughts, so strong they almost keep out the sound of the pneumatic drills *brr*-ing outside.

Eight

I've been invited to *her* party. All the girls have had little pink cards with roses on them and the boys blue ones with footballs – yuck, I thought, looking at mine. Lucy Chinn's party – in a stretch limo! She is *sooo* spoiled.

They come round the corner of the cloakroom, legs swishing, chatter, chatter. I hide under someone's smelly blue bag and listen.

'I've even invited BOYS,' Lucy's boasting, throwing back her head.

'Really?' exclaims Sally breathlessly.

'You must wear your best clothes. Everyone is coming and we're having *three* stretch limos.'

Everyone's talking about her party. Limos! Tarty clothes – Yuckkkk – I'm not going. I can't stand the idea.

Back in the classroom. Ryan's there choosing whatever

seat he fancies, laid-back, looking as if he's never been away. Boris, pale, panda circles round his eyes, is gazing at him as if he's a world-class footballer or President of the USA. (NB. Query: thought travellers' kids or gypsy kids – that's what Boris is – would be big and tanned. But he's little and pale.)

And we have – wait for it – a new teacher, not ole Warpole, not Mr Merchant, Sir, but a pretty one with cropped black hair and sexy specs. I hope she doesn't get pregnant like the last young and pretty one we had as that's how we came to get ole Warpole. Poor him. Poor us. She's called Miss Beattie! Doesn't suit her.

As well as looking like a ghost, Boris is very raggedy. Strawberry says she's got an idea about this, so can we meet up at lunchtime, after the literacy and Maths thrill time?

So we do, Shahid and me, Matthew, Rod and Ryan. His fan club are looking a tad let down, wondering when he's going to leap around being King Tarzan of the school, but he's staying very quiet and I think he just wants to brood like Hamlet on the unfairness of life. Boris is also there looking dazed.

Strawberry is saying she'd like to get him some school gear and stuff if he didn't mind, as he's only got rags and tags and he's being got at by some other kids, and if he didn't think we were horrible and snobby we could bring him whatever was going spare at home.

37

'No need,' Ryan says. 'Leave it with me!' He's chewing a grass stem – we're in the wild garden bit – and he walks off and comes back with Violet, who didn't take long returning to school, saying she'd missed us kids and the teachers.

'Come on,' she tells us. 'And quiet with it!'

We follow her, trying to look as if we're doing a survey for an important project, and there I am once more creeping into the big underground storeroom with Violet (and the rest).

'Stay there,' she says, so we all stay, woof woof, very good dogs, except for Rod who's quietly nicking bits and pieces, while she goes right into the dark dungeon bit at the back and Boris gets the shivs as we wait for her among all the old school junk from past happenings.

'It's awful spooky here,' he says. 'It scares me!'

But then he looks as if all the school scares him.

Then Violet and Ryan bring out a huge, bulging, broken cardboard box overflowing with blazers, shirts, plimsolls, bags, sports kit, trousers, pencil cases, trainers, footballs, felt tips and rubbish.

'Lost property. Way back. Nobody ever claims it. Might as well come in useful.'

She soon kits Boris up. Not bad, for some of the clothes are nearly new. He wriggles a bit and then we come out blinking into bright sunlight and Violet shoves the box of lost property to the back once more except for a scarf pinched by Rod. Violet doesn't notice this.

'We might get into a row for this,' moans Matthew. 'I don't like it much.'

'No, nobody wants all that stuff, honest,' Violet says.

'You don't think I look a bit funny?' asks Boris nervously.

'Not as bad as you did before. In fact you look OK.' Strawberry dusts his shoulders, then swings round and kisses Violet and Ryan.

'You're great,' she grins at them.

'Thanks,' mutters Boris, then says, 'You're not really wicked, are you, Ryan?'

'Oh, yes, I am. Aren't I, Snaggle?'

'Sure. Evil and wicked.'

'He's really a saint,' laughs Strawberry. 'St Ryan.'

'Then why were you . . . what's the word?'

'Excluded,' I help out.

'You really want to know? I was accused of trashing a car. An' I didn't do it!'

'Didn't you tell them?'

'Yes. Over and over again. And no one believed me. Mr Merchant and ole Warpole were away, the new Head Teacher hadn't arrived and Mrs Horrible Somers went on and on at this meeting and no one would stand up to her . . . And she said she had a witness who'd seen me, but she wouldn't say who it was, and in the end . . . '

Ryan is talking faster and faster, face red, eyes blazing. And I'm listening hard 'cos he doesn't usually talk much. Dare I? Dare I put this in the *Chronicle*? 'No' is the answer. But I'd like to. I could always ask him. Nothing ventured, nothing gained.

' . . . I got so mad I called her a stupid cow and that was it – the end – me finished – she said I'd always been a wicked boy, a bad influence and I'd be excluded for as long as she decided. And it would be put on my record for ever and ever. Excluded, Ryan Tiler, for vandalism and wilful damage to a car. And for bad language.'

All the colour leaves his face and he looks sick, green.

'But why?'

'She hates me. Hates all my family. Anybody called Tiler. Something that happened once here at this school. She was mixed up in it.'

Boris said, 'But that's unfair.'

'What's fair? You tell me, kiddo.'

The bell rings. It's time to go to class.

'But what about the police? What did they say?'

'I was cleared. They soon found out it wasn't me. I was in the Art room. Had an alibi. But *she* didn't believe me and said I'd still got to be excluded because

40

of my language and attitude. Mr Merchant came back this week and he put in a good word and ole Armpit wanted me for Games and Athletics, he told the new Head Teacher. So here I am.'

Ryan stops as we go into the classroom.

'I'll find out, you know. Find out who sneaked on me.'

'What about the trashed car?' asks Boris.

'They still don't know. Maybe they never will. But I'll find out. I promise. I promise,' answers Ryan. 'Then look out. I'll trash them.'

(Who did it? The biggest query OF ALL TIME? And can Ryan do it? We'll help him. The kids'd help Ryan do anything.)

Nine

I've done my best to get out of it, but still I've ended up here on Lucy Chinn's doorstep ringing the bell. She answers beaming. She's wearing purple velvet with fluffy white fur and silver hearts all over it and a diamond thing on her head. She's towering over me as she's wearing silver boots with ten-inch heels.

'Here,' I mutter, shoving an envelope at her. I dunno what's in it. Mum got it as I said I wasn't going to buy a present for Lucy Chinn even if they tortured me. My mother told me not to talk rubbish, and to remember to say 'Happy Birthday' when I handed over the envelope. This I just cannot manage. There are limits. I've turned up, haven't I? What more could anyone ask? So I leer my snaggletooth at her and watch while she opens the envelope. There's a book token inside.

'Oh, lovely,' she shrills at me. 'I'll spend it some time, but honestly, honestly, I get very little time to read. I'm into so many things! Of course, I look at the

Chronicle. You've made it really exciting. I do hope you give me and my party the front page. I've got a new camera for you to take my photo. Come on in.'

The room's full of tarty girls and boys trying to look cool and Lucy's prezzies – a camcorder, cassette players, CDs, make-up boxes, a Playstation and a mobile – that's just a few. In place of honour, tra-la-la, is a huge blonde doll dressed up as a twin of Lucy. You don't have to believe this if you don't want to. It's *sooo* disgusting.

I try not to be sick. But I now know why I've been invited. She wants to be in the *Chronicle*, does she?

'The limos are here,' her Dad announces, stepping into the crowded room. He's wearing a jeweller's shop, bracelets, two watches, earrings and a huge medallion nestling in the hairs on his chest.

I'm put in the first limo with her and the Girl Gang. Ryan's also there, so cool, I hear Santia murmuring to Sally.

I'm working hard on not looking impressed. The girls are cooing and ahhing and isn't it wonderful, isn't it grand, you're such a lucky girl, Lucy. Cool Ryan looks out of the window. I could be impressed, but I won't be, not me. Not Snaggle. I do things like riding in limos all the time, ha, ha. Blue velvet carpet, white leather seats, TV sets on the wall, soft music playing.

'Everyone take their shoes off,' Lucy commands. So

we do. Except Lucy, who keeps on her boots. It's probably a morning's work getting them on or off. The chauffeur's treating Lucy like she was Queen of the Month (tart of the month, more like it).

'Yes, Miss Lucy. No, Miss Lucy.'

I clamber to the window. The girls are flirting with Ryan, showing off. Disco music pounds off the stereo and I click my fingers to the beat and the window rolls down. I click again and it goes up. I just manage to stop myself saying 'Wow!'

And it's so funny watching people out of the window, craning their necks to see who's in the stretch limo. Pop stars? Celebrities? No, *moi*.

We drive on through the main streets, on and on, past the shops and offices, and then it seems all in a moment to change, as we turn a corner, and suddenly we're in a rough area, littered broken-up streets, some barbed wire, dumped cars, boarded-up houses and a burnt-out van, heaps of rubble. Another world. Then further on, a bridge and trees and a couple of gypsy caravans – not vans. Horses and ponies, two piebald.

And there in a stretch of rough grass is Boris throwing a stick for a three-legged dog and wearing his old rags and tags. 'Boris,' I yell, but of course he can't hear. I click my fingers and the window rolls down.

'Boris,' I yell, head stuck out one side. 'Boris, is that your dog?'

Lucy is shrieking her head off. 'Snaggle! Don't do that! He looks disgusting! Driver, take us home. NOW! I want to go home. We weren't supposed to be here! Home, driver.'

'Boris,' I yell once more, before she clicks up the window.

I know he sees me. The funny three-legged dog barks. But Boris turns away. He doesn't want to know. And the driver swings round the car back to Lucy's house.

'You shouldn't have done that, Snaggle! Don't you think, Ryan?'

He stuffs his hands in his pocket and shrugs, another one who doesn't want to know.

'People like him shouldn't be allowed,' went on Lucy. 'Spoiling my birthday. It's not fair. I don't want my birthday spoiled!'

She's still talking as we reach her house and get out of the car, as her fat white long-haired cat oozes out of the door and pads down the path towards us.

THE CRICKLEPIT CHRONICLE

THE EYES – THE EARS – THE VOICE – OF THE SCHOOL

Editor
Snaggletooth Watson

Assistant Editor
Shahid Malik

Reporter
Strawberry Rainbird

Exclusive!
Interview with
Ryan Tiler
&
MORE GHOSTLY NEWS

INTERVIEW WITH RYAN TILER

Ryan Tiler returned to school last week.
Strawberry Rainbird interviewed him.

Strawberry: Tell us, why were you excluded from school?

Ryan: Someone trashed Mrs Somers' car and she said it was me.

Strawberry: And had you?

Ryan: No! I was in the Art room at the time.

Strawberry: Then why did she say it was you?

Ryan: She has always hated me and she said someone saw me do it. She doesn't like anyone called Tiler. She says they cause trouble.

Strawberry: What is your record in this school?

Ryan: Well . . . er . . .

Strawberry: I'll do it for you. You're captain of football — we won the City Schools' Cup because of you. You play the drums in the school orchestra and you sang solo at Christmas. You won the Maths prize last year.

Ryan: Oh, shut up. I get by. And I don't trash cars.

Strawberry: OK, we'll leave that. You have a good record. Then why should somebody sneak on you?

Ryan: I dunno. They must hate me too, I suppose.

Strawberry: What did you do while you were excluded?

Ryan: Nuthin'. I mooched around, doing nuthin' much except watch telly and play computer games. My Gran came and she wouldn't let me go out in case I got into trouble.

Strawberry: Did you meet any other excluded kids? Meet any crime, shoplifting, vandalism, drugs, all that?

Ryan: No.

Strawberry: Did you really swear at Mrs Somers?

Ryan: No. But I was rude as it was unfair.

Strawberry: One last question. Do you want to find out who did trash the car?

Ryan: Yes, but not as much as I want to know who told lies about me. *Then, then*, I'll trash *them*.

INTERVIEW ENDED

LOCKED DOORS MYSTERY

GHOSTS AT CRICKLEPIT

The mystery of the locked doors at Cricklepit School continues. Yesterday the office door was shut tight for an hour, causing chaos, Mr Figgis, the school secretary said. Mr Figgis was very harassed and throwing his hair and hands around. Previously, Mr Warpole's classroom door was shut and Mr Warpole got a head injury falling down the stairs. He will be retiring early at the end of term. Mr Figgis is also thinking of leaving, he said. Two other doors have stuck for no reason, one in the teachers' cloakroom, the other in the staffroom where a lot of Head Teachers were with Mrs Markham and the Chief Education Officer!

Mrs Markham says that new locks are being fitted and she hopes that this will sort out the problem. Just leave doors open for now, if you can, she says.

Mrs Markham said at Assembly that there are no such things as ghosts, least of all at Cricklepit School. Take no notice of silly stories, she went on. She didn't wish any child to be frightened or put off their work.

Several children, including some in the top year, have seen the ghosts, they say. They are described as a boy and a girl, thin and pale and raggedy, holding hands and wandering about sadly. Teggy Watson in Year 3 says she sees them all the time. Some are old ghosts, she says, but these two are new ghosts. Most of them are friendly, she says. They float about and she talks to them sometimes. Mariella Higgins, her friend, says this is all true.

However, they will not tell us what they say so the *Chronicle* says it's best to take no notice of them.

END OF TERM CELEBRATIONS

Rehearsals for the End of Term concert will take place in the lunch hour. Please volunteer if you want a part or to play in the orchestra. There will be a poster competition.

CHESS CLUB

Shahid Malik and Ryan Tiler have reached the City semi-finals.

FOOTBALL

Ryan Tiler scored the winner against Northwood School. Rod Stringer and Matthew Ernest were sent off playing for the reserves who lost 5–1.

CRICKET

Cricklepit First beat Blundell's Junior by 126 runs to 94. Shahid Malik and Ryan Tiler made 85 between them. Matthew Ernest scored 5, Barry Morse 22.

ORPHANS OF AFRICA FUND

Strawberry Rainbird will be coming to your classroom collecting for the Orphans. Please give or bring what you can. Books especially welcome.

FOR SALE

Matthew Ernest has two lop-eared rabbits for sale. Snaggle Watson has 20 gerbils for sale (assorted colours).

Rod Stringer has 25 Pokemon cards. Fair prices.

WANTED

Gran Turismo 2 Playstation game. See Rod Stringer.

CONGRATULATIONS

Lucy Chinn gained a distinction in her Dance Exam Grade 4.

Sally Fox passed in Dance Exam Grade 1.

Tegwyn Watson and Mariella Higgins passed Trumpet exams Grade 2 with distinction.

GOSSIP

Lucy Chinn held a large party attended by most of her class. Anyone wanting a photo will have to ask her. The *Chronicle* was unable to print it.

Sally Fox has dumped Rod Stringer. He is now dating Lulu Sercombe. Rumours say he fancied Strawberry Rainbird but she told him to get lost though he could help her with collecting for Orphans of Africa providing he didn't nick anything!

Lucy Chinn claims she is Ryan Tiler's girlfriend. He denies this. He dumped her before and nothing has changed, he says.

Contributions for Mr Warpole's leaving present to be given to Miss P. Farthing. He has taught here for 31 years. Wow! Please give generously for someone who must have put up with kids bravely.

Ten

━━━━━━━━

I've got to have a brace for my tooth, my mother says, and my Dad drags me off to the dentist who is called Mr Torch – short for torture, I suppose.

'I do not want to have a brace! Who cares if my tooth sticks out? Not me! Besides, I like it. It's ME! *MOI!* I can't be Snaggle, Editor, with a brace!'

'You should have straight teeth,' says Dad.

'Why?'

'To look . . . nice, I suppose.'

'But I don't want to look nice. Who cares if I look nice? Who cares what anybody looks like? What you look like *doesn't matter*. It's what you're like inside that counts . . .'

'Oh, do be quiet, Snaggle! You never stop talking.'

'That's not fair. I don't talk any more than . . .'

'SHUT UP!'

'Well, if you're going to be rude, I won't say another

word. But you really needn't bother to take me to the dentist to get a brace . . . '

'SNAGGLE!'

Here I stand at Mrs Markham's door. It says 'HEAD TEACHER, Mrs Markham', with all her letters after her name, which is not very encouraging to someone like me who has been told to report to her, and *not* told why. I knock, very softly, hoping she isn't there. Not a murmur. I knock again, very gently, and if no one answers she obviously isn't in and I can go away and come again later. Not a stir. I'm just turning to go, humming the Number One to myself for comfort, when the door opens and there she is – a little person, but full of power, like Napoleon or Hitler or Queen Victoria, I suppose. No bigger than me, really, and I'm only half Ryan's size – or Lucy Chinn's, for that matter. (Query: are small people more intelligent as they don't waste so much time and effort growing?)

'You wanted to see me?' she asks.

'No, not really. Sorry, I didn't mean that. It just came out. Our new teacher said you wanted to see me.'

'Oh, yes, come in. Sit over there.'

I'm really nervous now. She looks stern and headteachery. I read a title – *Discipline in the Primary School* – on the bookcase at the back of her head. Next to it are *Curriculum Fun for Slow Learners* and *Loving*

Prayers for Assemblies. That's what I need. A loving prayer. This is not like going before Mrs Somers, Chair. Mrs Markham is an important, serious person, I think. Mrs Somers is stupid, like Ryan says.

'When you get your brace we shall have to stop calling you Snaggle, I suppose,' she starts off.

'I don't want my brace. I don't like changing things.' I sniff so I won't cry. What a morning!

'The *Cricklepit Chronicle* came out yesterday. And Strawberry delivered my copy.'

'Yes?' Trouble is waiting for me, I know.

'And Shahid gave a copy to Mrs Somers who was with us yesterday.'

'She's always here.'

'Mrs Somers is a most conscientious and indefatigable governor.'

'You mean hard-working, ma'am. And horrible,' I add under my breath.

'I didn't hear that.' She carefully *doesn't* smile. 'Now, I'll come to the point. I know that you, Shahid and Strawberry have worked very hard this year on the *Chronicle* and it is a credit to you. And it's well produced and printed. Your charge of 2p seems reasonable . . . '

'What's wrong then?'

'Briefly. Mrs Somers objects strongly to the interview with Ryan Tiler and the references to her. She says that she has told you before about going too far and writing about things you shouldn't.'

She continues, 'I'm also not too happy about your little sister's remarks about ghosts. I think it could create an atmosphere in the school that we don't want. On the other hand I do know that schoolchildren always talk about ghosts even though they have no reason to do so. It goes with their liking for horror stories, I suppose. So that doesn't worry me too much.'

She pauses, then, 'However – and I come to the point. Mrs Somers wants all the copies collected in and shredded.'

'But that's wicked! Awful people burn and destroy books and newspapers! Saddam Hussein, the Nazis – witch-hunting people!'

'You're well informed.'

'I read newspapers and I watch programmes. And my parents belong to Amnesty. You know, stopping people being tortured for what they believe in! Though I wish they wouldn't torture *me* with a brace!'

'This is an interesting discussion. However, I have to end it by saying you *must* collect all the copies in and bring them to Mr Figgis to be shredded. Now, I have some parents to see, so you can return to your classroom now. Snaggle . . .'

'Yes.' I'm sniffling hard now. All that work!

'I'll be very happy to receive your next *Chronicle*.

Just don't write anything about Mrs Somers! Then it will be all right. Oh, she also says the school computers and printers are not to be used for it.'

'We do them at our homes, anyway. Nothing to do with her.'

'Goodbye, Snaggle.'

She smiles at me and I guess she's OK, really.

Ages and ages it takes at lunchtime to get them back. The money is kept for the next one, which will be free. We keep back a lot of them and I hide some to take home with me. We can't bear to shred them all. Then we carry the ones we've got left to Mr Figgis to be shredded.

He is standing outside the office, stamping his feet, waving his head and shouting at the door which won't open, using a lot of strange words, some of them foreign, I think.

We plonk down the papers and vamoose fast, as I've had enough of doors that won't open.

But later we hear on the school grapevine that when the door *is* opened, all the SATs tests that were lying on top of the filing cabinet in an envelope have disappeared. Mr Figgis doesn't get around to shredding the *Chronicles*. A message comes to our classroom that no mention must be made of the missing SATs tests in the next *Chronicle*, or else . . .

'It's disgusting,' cries Lucy Chinn. 'I know I did well. So they mustn't get lost!'

'It's disgusting,' echo the Girl Gang.

'It's brill,' says Rod. 'I couldn't answer anything. I'm really chuffed they're missing. Maybe they're gone for good.'

Eleven

Searches for the SAT papers are being carried out all over the school, but quietly and secretly, in case too many people start to ask questions and trouble is stirred up. My guess is that no one wants Mrs Somers to find out about the papers disappearing, as she'll create merry hell shrieking about lack of care and efficiency and she'll tell everybody what they ought to do. Mr Merchant takes Strawberry, Shahid and me on one side and tells us that on no account are we to report it in the *Chronicle* – on pain of death, he adds, slitting his eyes at us.

'That's censorship,' I tell him. 'This is supposed to be a free school in a free city.'

'Snaggle, please give me a break!'

'Is something going on, Sir?' asks Shahid.

'I don't know. All I do know is that this is a funny term with a weird atmosphere, beginning with that car being vandalised. Never sorted out properly, you know. We don't know who did it. The police don't either.'

'What sort of atmosphere do you mean?' Shahid goes on.

'Well, there's the locked doors for a start. And Ryan going around like Sherlock Holmes asking questions everywhere.'

Ryan's going round school asking who trashed the car and who sneaked on him and saying he's thinking of offering a reward.

'And your sister Teggy doesn't help.'

'Oh, her! You don't want to take any notice of her. She's nuts,' I say.

'Well, she's got a trail of little kids following her all around the school asking her to tell their fortunes and to get the ghosts to talk to *them*. So they're all hyped up and noisy and shrieky and their teachers are complaining. Oh, don't write all this in your famous rag, will you?'

'Famous, Sir? Is it?' FAME! FAME! FAME! FAME! All I've ever wanted!!!

'Oh, yes. We get parents reading it at the school gates. I'm told the gossip column is popular so take care what you write.' He looks at his watch. 'It's time to go in. I'm with your class this afternoon, and you're about to have a further instalment of Life In Our Fair City as lived by the Victorian poor.'

'Can't wait, Sir,' grins Strawberry.

'Look out or I'll have you writing out spellings all afternoon. Blindfolded.'

'Red flannel belts,' announces Sir, as soon as we are settled in the classroom. I look at Strawberry who is rolling her eyes and tapping her forehead. I nod to show that I agree with her and that it is time Sir was put out to graze quietly with the old tired donkeys in the sanctuary near here. Poor old thing. We'll visit him. But he continues:

'7,695 red flannel belts were made and distributed to all the different parishes of the city. Our parish – where our school is now – received the largest number, 1,600 red flannel belts. Now, why do you think large quantities of red flannel belts were handed out in that dreadful, hot July of 1832?'

I look round at blank faces. Not a clue. Silence, silence, silence.

'What was happening in July 1832?'

The silence is embarrassing. Come on, Snaggle. So I beat Shahid by half a second.

'Cholera.'

'They used red flannel belts to frighten away the cholera,' says Lucy Chinn.

'To make them look nice when they stayed in bed,' adds Sally Fox.

'You don't care how you look when you're dying of cholera, stupid,' snaps Ryan. His temper's rotten these days.

'They probably got the shivers and red flannel belts helped to keep them warm,' says Shahid.

'That's it. The temperature of the sufferers dropped alarmingly and the authorities hoped the warmth of the flannel would help them to recover. Now why do you think we had more distributed here than anywhere else?'

'The cholera was worst here?'

'Yes.'

'Why?'

'Is it because it was the poorest parish?'

'Very good, Strawberry. Yes, it was. And more people died here than anywhere else in the city. Now, you're going to get to your feet, and follow me quietly to the school gates with no fuss at all, and look around the street running next to your school. Oh, this isn't a school trip to Alton Towers or Disneyland so there's no need for wild excitement. I just want you all to look at something.'

We stand on the pavement outside the school railings. The afternoon's hot, sleepy. Cars are parked everywhere in the narrow street, outside the 'Saucy Plaice', the Kasbah, the Oxfam shop, and the shop selling stained glass that is made in the workshop behind. Above the shops are houses and flats and above them more houses crowded together on the steeply rising ground.

'What are we supposed to be looking at, Sir?' asks Matthew.

'We'll cross at the pedestrian corner crossing, then walk along the pavement by the shop till I tell you to stop.'

So we do.

'He's flipped,' I whisper to Strawberry. 'Definitely due for the funny farm. There's nothing here unless we're going to have a lesson on Chinese cuisine.'

'Snags, I've been meaning to ask you,' she whispers. 'Yeah?'

'Boris. He's not here. And he wasn't here yesterday.'

'Mitching, I 'spect.'

'Stop here,' cries Sir. 'And tell me what you see.'

'I can see a new silver Focus like the one Mum's boyfriend's just got,' answers Rod. 'But I like the Land Rover better.'

'No, Rod, not the cars. Something else. Look again.' He points and at last we see a small opening in a narrow space between two shops. There's a pattern set in a curve above a tiny stone bowl. We gather round and try to look astonished.

'Once all the city water came from a spring under

here.' (No, I don't believe it.) 'What's this street called?'

'Well Street.' We all know *that* one.

'*Well* named! As early as 1221 all the city water, except from the river, was taken from here to the Cathedral and the big houses in the centre. Much later there wasn't enough, but first of all it came from here. How? Next week we'll find out. Now, let's get back to the classroom.'

We drag Rod away from the cars and get back to school.

Twelve

It's near the end of the afternoon and I'm in the entrance hall outside the office, pinning up a notice about the next *Chronicle* and thinking I'd like to ask Figgie if the SATs papers have been found yet, when there's a ring on the bell and Figgie rushes out of the office, hair and hands going like a windmill.

Three people and a dog enter – Boris's three-legged dog – and they are Boris and his mother and grandmother, I think. His mother has an orange-and-purple Mohican and is wearing a very long cloak thing over a very short skirt and wrinkled boots. The old lady is in black and carrying a basket full of plants, pegs, trinkets and ribbons. Her head is wrapped in hundreds of tight grey-black plaits, round and round and round. She fixes Figgie with her black eyes and says, 'Take me to the Head.'

'Yes, of course,' replies Figgie in his posh Oxford

accent. 'Who shall I say it is?' He's trembling. They are pretty scary. (But interesting.)

'It's us,' answered the old lady, very dignified. Off he goes.

I look busy taking my notice down as I don't want to miss this. Boris is pale and I grin at him to show I'm right there with him, but he just twitches a bit. The dog comes and sniffs round me. He's on a long piece of string.

But before Figgie can return with Mrs Markham in tow, the door combination is worked and, phew, in bangs herself, Mrs Somers, in full Boadicea style. She immediately fixes on the grandmother and they both draw themselves up to their full heights (about up to Mr Figgis's knees), and stick out their fat chests.

'Who are you? What are you doing here?' she barks.

'And who are you?' the old lady hisses. She's much more scary than Mrs Somers, I think.

'I am Chair of Governors.'

'And I'm the cat's whiskers' goes through my head, but of course I don't say it. Boris, the dog and me slip back into a corner as battle is about to take place.

'And I am here to see the Head about this DISGUST-ING SCHOOL!' The whisper suddenly grows to a roar, just as we are joined by Mrs Markham and Figgie. The entrance hall is now crowded. I draw Boris, who brings Three-Legs with him on to the bottom stairs

64

which lead to Spooky Land and the Haunted Staff-room and Cloakroom . . . we know where.

'You wish to see me?' asks Mrs Markham.

But before Boris's Gran can answer, Mrs Somers shouts, 'What are persons like this doing in *our* school? Cluttering up the hall? Look at that dreadful dog!' she shouts. 'Get it out of here!'

Boris, me and the dreadful dog retreat and go two further steps up – on our bums. Boris looks haunted. I'm not surprised.

'Please come into my room where we can talk in peace,' says Mrs Markham.

'Be careful, ma'am,' cries Mrs Somers. 'Who knows what these (sniff, sniff) people are carrying with them?'

Does she mean fleas, knives, Aids, BSE, rabies, foot-and-mouth, bubonic plague, CHOLERA (yuck)? I wonder. (NB. Query: how many plagues do visitors bring into school? You can't keep them out with fancy locks.)

The old lady is ready for her.

'Ah, now I understand. All is revealed to me.' She lifts her basket high. A roll of ribbon flutters down and I hold back Boris from rushing to pick it up.

'We – my daughter Persephone and I – came to complain about the bullying that our Boris has suffered. But now I'm here I see that it is useless to

65

hope that we could stop this yet. For there is a curse . . . '

She lifts her other arm in the air – then waves it round (no, not the one holding the basket) and points straight at Mrs Somers who backs to the front door.

' . . . upon this place. There was sorrow and sin here . . . '

'Still is,' I whisper to Boris.

' . . . but for years the sin and sorrow lay quiet. But now sin and sorrow stir again BECAUSE OF THE EVIL EYE!'

And her finger points directly at the Chair of Governors, Mrs Somers, who is choking with rage, gag, gag, gag.

Mrs Markham stays calm. 'I think it would be better if we discussed all this quietly in my office.'

'No, no, no. I cannot stay here. For here are ghosts and doom. Ghosts and doom. All around us as we stand here.'

I look round nervously. That accounts for it, then, I think. (NB. Article on gloom, doom and ghosts in the *Chronicle*. That should sell a few.)

'But the worst thing is this creature here! This Chair woman! She must go!'

'If you don't get out of here, I'll call the police,' grits Mrs Somers through her clenched teeth, fury lifting her up on her toes.

'You needn't bother,' cries Boris's grandma, Mystic Meg. 'We're leaving this Unhappy, Doomed Place! Persephone! Boris!'

Boris shakes his head and clutches me, hiding his head in my shoulder, as the dog tries to climb on my lap, not easy with his three legs. Suddenly they're all looking at US!!! Oh, no.

And Violet comes in. It looks like the Three Witches of Cricklepit, with Mrs Somers, Violet, and Boris's grandmother.

'All having a little party, then? I was just going to tidy up for end of the afternoon. Sorry, ma'am, I didn't see *you* were there. They're cleaning up in your classroom, Snaggle. It must be time to go home!'

I'm hit with an idea.

'My mum says Boris can come to tea,' I say to his ma and grandma. 'We'll bring him home later!'

And we get the hell out of there as fast as we can, hauling the three-legged pooch after us.

Thirteen

'Did your mother really ask me to tea?' says Boris as we escape from school. 'I've never been asked to tea before.' He's stopped trembling, but he is *sooo* scared all the time.

'Well, you haven't now. But it doesn't make any difference. Our house is always full of kids. And Mum won't be in anyway as she's at work. Dad'll be there somewhere. He works from home.'

Ryan and Shahid catch up with us and we race back home kicking Ryan's bag (he even kicks a bag better than the rest of us) and we visit all our animals – dog, cat, rabbit, hamsters, gerbils. Then we play footie with Kris (who wears earrings and has a shaved head), Mizza and Cameron on the bomb site, as Dad calls it – he says someday he's gonna get the Garden Army to bulldoze it flat and have it landscaped. In your dreams, Dad, in your dreams, grins Mizza, who plays footie better than any of us, except Ryan. Romilly joins in, surprise, surprise, as she's all teenage glam and too posh for us usually. Ryan's team wins, boring, boring.

Cameron shows them where he had his nipple pierced. He got in an awful row and lost his pocket money.

'Where's your Dad?' asks Ryan when we go on a grub search in the kitchen.

'He always hides in his room when we're all here. Says he created a universe he can't cope with.'

'I don't know what you mean, but there's an awful lot of you. What's their names?' asks Boris.

'Romilly (the posh git – she's horrible), Mizza and Cass are Dad's, Kris and Cameron are Mum's. They're OK. Me and Teggy are both Dad's *and* Mum's. We're the lucky ones, if you can call it that. You got a brother or anything?'

'There's Mum and Gran. But all of us at the camp are all one family really, only Gran's the boss.'

'I can see that. I like your dog. What's he called?'

'Ramses.' (Ramses is playing with our dog, Boxie.)

'Hey! That's cool.'

'I don't know about cool. It's our sort-of gypsy name.'

Everybody's doing their own thing. Ryan and Cass have wandered off together, snogging, I guess. Cass is dishy, yummy, they say. Lucy Chinn, you don't stand a chance. Cass is two years older. And clued.

Ryan really goes for her. Music's going everywhere as well.

Dad appears and shouts, 'Shut up there! I can't hear myself think.' He goes back to his den, slamming the door.

I go to take Boris to show him *my* room and *my* books, and there sitting in the middle of the stairs, right in the way of anybody going up or down, is Teggy, talking to Mariella and someone else who isn't there.

'Hi, Boris,' Teggy says. 'Meet Grandad.'

'Hi, Grandad,' says Boris, holding out his hand and lifting it up and down, which looks silly and makes me feel very ill. Not another one!

'Shut up, Teggy! And you, Face-ache!'

'Shut up yourself, Gobby-mouth, Toothy-woothy, Wobble-gob. Grandad's talking to Boris.'

'Come on, Boris. Take no notice of them. They're crazy. Come on.'

But Boris takes no notice of *me*. He sits down on the stairs, and for the first time since I've known him, he looks happy, talking and smiling.

At last he looks round at me – I'm sitting on the stairs waiting, trying not to listen.

'Snaggle! He knows all about it. Your Grandad.'

'Boris. My Grandad is dead.' I speak slowly to let it sink in.

'But he says he knows what's wrong . . .'

' . . . told you,' chimes Teggy.

'Hold it! Please! I don't want to know. Not from Grandad, anyway.'

And like a miracle Dad appears. 'If you want me to drive your friend whatsisname, we'll go now – I've got to go out soon. Have you done your homework?'

'Oh, NO! I left it in school. Sorry, Dad. All that rush. In the cloakroom.'

'You would. Look, I'll run you and your mate home – drop you off at school and pick you up on the way back.'

'Oh, yes, yes. Thank you, Dad, yes.'

'Goodbye, Grandad,' Boris says as I hurry him away, still smiling. 'See you again.'

Muttering, I get Ryan away from Cass and Shahid, away from the Playstation, and leap in the car. (NB. Never mix friends and family. It doesn't work. The stress is horrible. And it's *sooo* embarrassing.)

In the car Boris bursts out with 'Grandad says . . .'

'Please, lad, whoever you are, I've forgotten your name, I'm sorry, but you seem nice enough – don't whatever you do get mixed up with Teggy and Grandad, for that is the road to madness, I tell you. I really tried to sort it out, but then I decided to leave her to it. So did Snaggle. Understand? The best thing is just to ignore her, or before we know where we are we'll have a tent in the garden and a crystal ball . . . '

'My Gran's got a crystal ball . . . '

'Look out, Dad, you nearly hit that car!'

'Sorry! Sorry! Crystal balls upset me, that's all. Have you got your seat belts fastened?'

'Yes, Dad.'

'Well, can we change the conversation?' he yells.

'It wasn't a ghost. It was Snaggle's Grandad. I saw him clearly. He was wearing a knitted pullover,' says Boris.

We touch the kerb as Dad swerves again, and I scream, 'Dad! Look out! We're here. Oh, let me out! I'll see you kids later.'

Boris tries to hang on to me. 'Snaggle – I must tell you. And Ryan. And Shahid . . . '

'Tomorrow'll do. OK?'

I jump out, run to the entrance and nearly crash into Violet just coming out of the front door.

'Look out! What you doing here?'

'I forgot my bag. It's in the cloakroom.'

'Well, it's getting quite late. I've finished and there's no one in school now. You're a nuisance, Snag.'

Seeing Violet makes me feel better.

'I know. I'm the Snag in your life.'

She looks at me blankly. 'Sorry, my little joke,' I mutter.

'Look, I've got my ole' man's supper to get and he turns moody if it isn't ready for him. Cyril needs a lot of supper.'

'I've seen him. He's ginormous.'

'Yeah, well, what I'm saying is, I'm off. I fixed the door. Just pull it shut behind you when you come out.'

'Leave it open. Please. I don't want to get shut in . . .'

'It'll be all right. I'll leave it a little way open. Then you pull it to when you go. See you, Snaggle.'

I shoot to the cloakroom, whistling. There's my bag. I check inside. The homework's there. No problem. I'll let myself out and wait for Dad. Easy-peasy. And there's masses of evening left to get my homework done. Back to the entrance hall.

The front door is shut. I stop whistling.

The fat thick silence blankets around me, smothering me. That silence. I can almost touch it. And then into that silence burrows the *brr brr brr* of the pneumatic drill, and I remember I haven't heard it for the last couple of days. Till now. Till now.

Deep breath. And again. Like Cass has shown me when she plays her saxophone. I couldn't make the wind sound like she does, but while I was still trying she taught me to breathe. Like athletes, she says, and it also stops panic attacks – panic, panic. I breathe slowly in and out while the silence seizes and crushes me. Breathe in, breathe out. Again. *Now* try the door.

I go to try the door . . . It won't open.

I try again. It still won't open.

I'M SHUT IN!!!

Bang, bang, bang, shove, push, pull, bang, pull, pull, pull, shout, shout . . . scream, scream.

'Help! Help! Let me out! Let me out! Get me out of here! PLEASE! Help!'

The sounds echo and fall away. To nothing, nothing, nothing, no-thing, no, no, o, zero, o, no. The *brr*-ing stops.

I'm alone in the school.

The silence and me.

Breathe in and out again, Snaggle.

OK. You're alone in the school, alone in the school . . . Don't mind. Come on. Be brave. Have some guts! Bottle! Don't be a wimp, chicken. Nothing can harm me if I'm alone in the school. But am I? Suppose, suppose I'm *not* alone in the school. And what could be in with me? THAT'S MY PROBLEM!

Who's there? Somebody's there? Something's there? I can feel it. A presence.

They say the school's patron saint, the martyr St Sativola, had her head chopped off at the Well – yes, *that* Well, that was once in Well Street when it was open fields. She went there to fetch water and her wicked stepmother, who hated her because she was a Christian, sent her servants there to ambush her and chop off her head.

Now I, me, *moi*, Snaggle, know that wicked step-mothers are unlikely. Stepdads are the *real* baddies, says Mum and grins *wickedly* at Dad. And Mr Merchant told us that Heads and Wells were part of the Celtic religion, so I don't know what I'm think-ing except that I'm here, alone, faced with a locked door and no escape. I remember Sally Fox crying once 'cos she said she'd seen the Saint in assembly, a Saxon lady carrying her head.

Suppose she's here in the school now, with me?

But isn't she supposed to look after children in the school? ME! She ought to. Perhaps she does. Me. Me. I need help. My head's spinning inside – help me, Saint. I'm sweating and the sweat's going cold. I'm so scared! What did Teggy say? New ghosts. So it wouldn't be St Sativola. New ghosts! Oh, no, no, no. Please. She also says *not all the ghosts are friendly*. Please let them be friendly.

I'm going crazy thinking like this. And the *brr brr* of the pneumatic drill is going again. Why is it *brr*-ing at this time of night? The men don't work at night. Is there really a drill? I haven't seen any near the school lately. Is that noise really something else – something strange? A fiendish monster ghost GRINDING ITS TEETH!?

Bang – crash – on door, bang – shout, bang-shout, bang-shout.

Don't leave me in here all night! Please! Snaggle, say a prayer – here goes.

'Dear St Sativola, and our Father . . .'

The doorbell rings.

The door opens.

Dad. Dad. Dad. Dad. And Violet. And Teggy.

I hurl myself at him and hug him as hard as I can till he squeaks.

'Hold on,' he says, unfastening himself. 'It's nice to be loved, but don't go over the top.'

'He forgot you and came back home,' Tegs says. 'So I *made* him come and fetch you 'cos I thought I heard you calling. And I made him get Violet to open the door.'

'Teggy, I love you.'

'I know *that*, silly. Come on.'

Fourteen

—————

Next morning I wake up not wanting to go to school. My head hurts. I ache all over. I feel rotten. I'm hot. Mum comes in to get me up and I tell her my temperature's up in the thousands. Rubbish, she says, after some horrible moments with the thermometer. (Query: what makes you want to bite it off in your mouth so much?)

After a century she takes it out.

'Nothing's wrong with you. Your uniform's ready on the chair.'

How can anybody, even a mother, be so unfeeling? Why are grown-ups so cruel? (NB. Article on grown-up cruelty? No, it would be too long.) Braces on teeth and now being sent to school when it's obvious I've got some terrible illness. Probably cholera. At the thought of cholera I twitch all down the bed. No, not cholera.

'But I don't wanna go.'

'Why not? Tell me. Is it your work?'

'Nah. S'awright. But I don't like school much right now. Crazy things going on.'

'What things?'

'Ryan's busy footing round school being Sherlock Holmes to find out who shopped him. And even if he's a star player he's a rotten detective. Kids giggle and run away. Lucy Chinn and the Girl Gang have got all the best parts in the end-of-term pageant and are showing off *all of the time* instead of just part of the time. And they keep taking the mickey out of Boris, and the other classes are getting at him as well. SATs are still missing and there's gonna be a row about it. Mrs Somers pokes her nose everywhere on the lookout for bad behaviour so she can get us reported, especially Ryan. And . . . and . . . and I don't want to have a brace!!!'

'Is that all? Any more problems?'

'Yes! Mum!' I clutch her hand. 'It's the ghosts. I know you don't believe in ghosts, but there's some funny things happening you can't explain.'

'Look, just get on with your work, Snaggle, and don't worry. Term'll soon be over and you'll be off to a new school. You'll probably never see Mrs Somers again. I know she's awful. Just keep out of her way. As for the ghosts . . . '

'Teggy says . . . '

'Teggy's very silly just now. Your father and I are going to have a talk with her. Don't take any notice of what she says. *There are no ghosts in your school!* Believe me. You're quite safe there as you have been for the last – how many? – six years. If a ghost had been going to get you it would've done it by now.'

'Yes, Mum.'

'Get up. Get washed. Get dressed. Get off to school. Quit worrying.'

'Yes, Mum. But I tell you, school's going crazy.'

'Well, take care *you* don't!'

She turns to go. I pull at her to stop her.

'Mum, I don't wanna go. There was something there with me in school last night, honest. I was so scared. And I do really feel ill.'

Mum turns at the doorway.

'There's a poem about a kid like you trying to get out of going to school . . .

> *I have the measles and the mumps,*
> *A gash, a rash and purple bumps.*
> *My mouth is wet, my throat is dry,*
> *I'm going blind in my right eye!*

Off you go, Snags! School!'

But I don't go *that* day after all. Mum goes to work and Dad's an old softy really, and so him and me, we

79

watch *Godzilla* together. It was FUN! Not scary. Not like *our* school ghost.

'I wish you'd be a school governor instead of Mrs Somers,' I say.

'Oh, I'd be no good. Your mother would be better.'

'Why won't she?'

'She saw all the work Grandad had to do when he was one, and said she'd never want to do it. Besides, she'd never have time.'

'Well, perhaps Mrs Somers'll get tired of it or there'll be a miracle. Have we got time for another video?'

'You're wicked, Snaggle. I should be working, you know.'

'So should I, so we're both wicked.'

Fifteen

'Find a partner!' Sir bellows, his words re-echoing throughout our small classroom. School trip (a mini one) and we'd been told that we'd need a packed lunch and some money about a week before. Of course, some of the dimwits in my class have forgotten both so they've got an absolutely GROSS school packed lunch (half a mouldy sandwich, a rotten apple and gone-off flapjack) and are given a tiny handout from school funds.

Lucy Chinn is choosing from a queue. Boris keeps trying to grab me to talk about Grandad, which I do not want to do, no, no, no-o-o-o so I team up with Shahid and talk very fast about nothing to him. (NB. Anything to do with my family is embarrassing.) And I'm keeping quiet about how scared I was in school.

Mr Merchant was vague in class about where we're going. He and Miss Beattie and Penny Farthing are coming too. I wonder which one he'll partner. Beattie is prettier, but Penny is more appealing. He walks between the pair of them – coward.

'No fancy shoes today,' he said earlier. 'It may be mucky.' When I heard that I'd perked up. That inspires me. So where? A bog pond? A railway station? An ancient house? A muddy graveyard? But no. Up town we go.

'We're here.'
  'Already?'

UNDERGROUND PASSAGES

I can hear Lucy talking loudly with the new upmarket voice she's taken to using lately. Yuck, yuck and double yuck.

Down a rusty iron staircase we go into a bright room with displays all over the walls, some about cholera. I read that the underground passages have been here since Roman times!

Find a document on the wall – *our* saint! Her story! ('Caw!' – as the crow said to the blackbird.) I knew some of it anyway. They tell it us in school, but I waded through it to check.

The story of the life of the Saint has been preserved in the

Cathedral for 500 years, but is clearly based on earlier material. It tells how a rich noble, by name Bonia, a Christian, who lived outside the City of Exeter, had one son and four daughters. The eldest daughter, Sativola, was a Christian, renowned for her 'beauty of form and blamelessness of behaviour'. After the death of her mother she incurred the enmity of her stepmother, who was a pagan. This stepmother induced the serfs who were mowing the meadows to the east of the City to set upon Sativola as she came down to bring them their food. Thus she was slain with a scythe, and where her head fell, there gushed out a 'most sparkling spring'. The date of her martyrdom is said to be AD 740. Some students would see in this story a much earlier legend connected with the corn spirit, and in all probability the fame of this spring dates back to before the coming of the Romans. It is sufficient for our purpose, however, to show that it must have been a well-famed spring in very early times. Water from this spring flowed through the underground passages to the Cathedral and the City.

Wow!

We walk down the rickety iron staircase and into another room with displays all over the brick walls. I read all of them – they keep mentioning cholera. We watch a video of the passages and then:

'Please follow me,' says the guide who's wearing a

name tag saying 'Tracey', only it sounds like 'Per-lease forlow me.'

We troop into another room with hard hats hanging up in rows and we each have to put one on.

At last, we're ready for off. We twist and turn down stone steps into the stone passages where once the city water flowed. It's dark, just a few dimly lit lights scattered here and there. And it's got a spooky, mysterious atmosphere, as if bad things had once happened there. (NB. Good copy here.)

'Eowh, I saw a rat!' shrieks Lucy, wrinkling her nose in distress.

The Girl Gang all shriek.

'It's only a stone,' says the guide. 'See?'

'Pass me a sick bag,' I whisper to Shahid.

Strawberry giggles next to us. Once she starts giggling she can't stop. I hit her gently to make her shut up, as the tour guide, Tracey, is giving us evil looks.

'Ssshh, listen,' I hiss, trying to concentrate on what she's saying.

'We will now turn out the lights so you can see what it would have been like for the people in the olden times.'

Click. Everything goes black.

'Oh! It's so dark!' Lucy squeals, playing the oh, oh, oh, damsel in distress.

Click. The lights come back on. I look at her and

notice that half the boys in the class are around her trying to comfort her. How they find their way to her I don't know. Unless they can smell her sickly sweet perfume. I certainly can – yuck!

'Who way-ould like to come down this very narrow passage – on hands and knees – to see how narrow it real-lie was?' asks Tracey.

Some of the boys and half the girls (not Lucy, she flinches at the thought of getting dirty) decide to go. And me.

It's certainly very, very narrow down there and almost completely black. I clamber after Shahid, hitting my head twice; Ryan nearly gets stuck – it isn't half cramped down here – until finally . . . daylight (yes!). I was glad to get out of there. We clamber out and shake ourselves off. Mud, stones and grit fly everywhere, covering the others, who aren't dirty. Good!

Our trip over, we say thank you to the guide and climb back up the steps, where Mr Merchant does a quick head count and frowns. Someone is missing. We're a head short.

After cries of 'It's Santia, Sir!' and 'No, it's Rod!' . . . 'No! It's Sally!' . . . 'No, I'm not missing, I'm here' . . . 'Only in the head' – it turns out to be Boris, of course.

'Snaggle – you're quick and little. You go and get him.'

I slowly (slowly because she seems dim) explain to the tour guide and she says she's too busy and I'll have to go look, see, on my own. I don't much want to, but I think about war correspondents and if I'm going to be one I've got to conquer my fears. (Even if I'm terrified? *Yes*!)

So I put the hat on and go into the dark unknown – and I can't find him. He's gone, disappeared, vamoosed. I say a word that Mrs Somers would not care to hear, and explore further, breathing a bit hard though I'm *not* afraid (much). It's light, even if I am on my own. But I'm fed up. (Query: do small people get bullied more than big ones? Yes, yes, yes.)

'Help! Help!'

It's coming from round the corner. Boris is in the dark, narrow tunnel. But where is he? I can't see him. I crawl on further – my knees will never feel like knees again – the tunnel floor here's not smooth stones but rocky rubble. I crawl on and on until I touch something hard and solid . . .

'Aaaaaahhhh,' the tunnel echoes, 'aaaahhhh, aaahhh.' It's Boris.

'What the heck are you doing here?'

'Somebody,' he whimpers, 'shoved me here and left me.' I touch his face and it's wet and snotty and crumpled.

'Who?'

'I dunno, do I?'

He's wedged into a corner. I pull him out into the passageway.

'What happened?' I ask, wiping my hands on my jeans, which doesn't help dry them.

'Some kids ... put a hand over my eyes and my mouth ... and pushed me in here. I banged my head and I couldn't call out for a minute and by then, you'd all gone and left me. But I thought you would come for me, Snaggle. Or Ryan. But he's too big. And I was scared a ghost might get me first. There's ghosts everywhere. Snaggle, I must tell you ... '

He sobs and sniffles and gulps.

'Oh, come on!' I grab his cold hand and pull him through the passageway until we reach daylight where they're singing:

> *Why are we waiting? We are suffocating.*
> *Why are we waiting? Oh, why, oh, why?*

OK. So we're a bit bored, are we? Well, I hope the kids who did that to Boris are *very very* bored. And worse. And if they don't stop bullying, I'll name and shame them in the *Chronicle*!!!

Boris is pulling at my sleeve, trying to tell me something. But I'm not listening.

Suddenly it pours down with rain so we hurtle back to school to eat our lunches, just as ...

Sixteen

. . . Dad is storming through the school gates. His face is like a black hole in the universe and he's dragging Teggy along so fast she can hardly keep her little fat feet on the ground and she's crying – Teggy, who hardly ever cries.

I rush over. 'What's up? What's the matter? Dad? Tegs?'

Dad takes absolutely no notice, just slams Teggy into the car and drives off leaving me gobsmacked, Teggy's face gazing pitifully after me out of the window, mouth turned down.

I grab at Sir's sleeve.

'What is it? What's happened? What's Teggy done? Sir, Sir, what's it all about?'

'I'm sure everything's all right, but I'll get Penny here to find out for you.'

'Teggy never cries. Dad never gets in a temper. Mum does. Not Dad. It'll be Mrs Somers,

I bet. Can I go home to find out, please, Sir?'

'No, that's *not* a good idea. Just wait here in the entrance hall while Penny finds out. It's probably nothing serious.'

Strawberry waits with me, 'cos that's what Strawberry does. I'm worried sick.

'Someone's died. Had an accident!' I shriek at her.

'No, they haven't. Teggy's just been naughty, that's all.'

'Penny's taking ages . . .'

A small figure creeps in to join us in the entrance hall.

'Mariella! What's going on? What's up? Tell me.'

Mariella looks round cautiously, fingers on lips. 'I'm not supposed to be here. I got into trouble as well. But Mrs Markham thought it was really all Teggy so she let the rest of us go. She was dead angry. You should've seen her, Snaggle. I've never seen her angry before. She took Teggy away . . .' She took a deep breath, ' . . . and then, I think, they phoned your Dad. I think she'll be exclu . . .'

'Excluded,' I finished for her. 'No, not Teggy! Surely! Anyway, what has she done? Kicked a teacher? Murdered somebody? Get on with it, Mariella.'

'You know that alphabet board game?'

'Alphabet board game? You crazy?'

'Stop shaking me, Snaggle, or I shan't tell you!'

'Sorry. What alphabet board game?'

'You put the alphabet letters all round the table and a "Yes" and a "No", then you turn a glass upside down and you all sit round and put your fingers on the glass and a spirit comes and pushes it round and round – sometimes it whizzes ever and ever so fast, Snaggle, and it tells you what you want to know. Teggy got your Grandad to be the spirit.'

'Oh, no,' I shriek.

'Shush,' Strawberry pats me gently. 'It's only a game.'

'No, it's not! She's been using a Ouija board . . . It's no game . . . '

'That's it, Snaggle. That's the name. And it tells you what's going to happen! Teggy asked about all the happenings here and the glass went whzz, whzz, whzz, all round the table so we could hardly keep our fingers on it. G-H-O-S-T-S, it spelt. I thought it was spelt G-O-S-T-E-S. Then she asked if it was the Saint.'

'Our school Saint?'

'Yes. But it wasn't. Cholera ghosts, it said. Whzz! Whzz! Cholera ghosts seemed to make it very cross and whzzy.'

Penny comes in and is going to say something, but listens to Mariella instead. Boris slides in behind her.

' "Tell us some more, please, Grandad," Teggy says, and whzz, whzz, whzz, Grandad says, cholera and water. "Cholera and water what?" says Teggy. In the school, whzz, whzz.'

'Oh, no. Oh, no.'

'I tried to tell you, Snaggle,' whispers Boris. 'But you wouldn't listen to me.'

'And then Mrs Markham walked in and everything blew up . . . '

Tears flow down Mariella's face.

'We're naughty, Snaggle. Strawberry, we're really wicked!' she sobs.

Penny takes her hand.

'Come on, Mariella, that's enough now. And you'd all better get along to your classrooms. I think Mrs Markham will be having a word with you. Teggy's safe at home, Snaggle. And your father and mother will be talking to you as well.'

Outside in the playground, nearly all the girls from Year 6 and Year 7 have linked hands and are swinging round and round, singing:

> We're the Girl Gang
> Leaders of the pack
> We're all things bright and beautiful
> Get a load of that!!!

Then I hear a mad roar as the soccer-playing mob rush in to break it up. But I'm not joining in. I want to go away and think. Before I go crazy.

Seventeen

I wake up not wanting to go to school. My head hurts. I ache all over. I feel rotten. I'm hot.

'No, not again,' Mum sighs, popping a thermometer into my mouth.

This time I'm not claiming my temperature's up in the thousands and she's not reciting poetry.

'It's high,' she says, after the mouth misery finishes. I know, but I can't be bothered to say so. I'm too tired even to think of the *Chronicle*. She draws back the curtains she drew open when she came in, and tells me to go back to sleep.

So I do.

I wake up for the doctor. Then after some tablets and a drink, I sleep again.

Dad's there. Sitting on a chair by my bed. I *must* be ill. I sleep.

Mum again. More tablets and drink.

'What day is it?'

'The day after yesterday,' says Dad. Glory, glory, he's there as well. I must be ill. Sleep.

It's Dad.

'What day is it?' after tablets and drinks.

'The day after the day after yesterday.'

'Where's Teggy?'

'Gone to stay with Granny. She's OK.'

'Not Gran who's dead!!!!'

'Of course not. What's the matter with you kids? Teggy's gone to stay with Granny Jenkins, your Mum's mum. *She'll* talk some sense into her. Long walks and multiplication tables for Madam Teggy, I think. Oh, don't get upset. Teggy's fine.'

'Want Cass.'

'Not yet. You might be infectious.'

'What's up with me?'

'Some sort of virus. Which means they don't know. You've got to rest, then you'll be OK, the doctor says.'

'It's not . . . not cholera?'

'OF COURSE IT'S NOT CHOLERA! Oh, sorry, I didn't mean to shout. No, there's something going round school, and a lot of children and teachers are absent. What are you crying for?'

'I'm not crying. But the old gypsy said . . . '

'Snaggle, I'm fond of you. I like you as well and better than some of this family that's somehow happened to me. BUT I don't want to hear anything more about ghosts, cholera, Grandad, old gypsy ladies – you understand, Snaggle?'

'Yes, Dad. Can I get up soon?'

'You can come down tomorrow, probably. Though why anyone should want to in this house beats me. It's cosy up here in your little attic on your own and you've got all your stuff here . . . '

'I still want to come down.'

'Tomorrow. The doctor's coming and he'll say when.'

I start to think about the *Chronicle*. And things.

Later.

'Dad, now I'm not infectious any more, I'd like to go to the reference library. Before I go back to school.'

'Yes, if that's what you want. What are you going to look up?'

'Oh, just something I'll have missed, being away.'

'Oh, all right. Don't tire yourself out, though. And don't worry about missing work – half the school's been absent, they tell me. But I'll take you.'

'Thanks, Dad.'

'I'm pleased you're using the library.'

You wouldn't be if you knew what I was looking up, I think. I can't use his computer because he's got a secret password to stop us lot going on the Internet after he nearly fainted from shock after one enormous phone bill. He'd thought it was a mistake at first, till he found out we'd all been surfing on it day and night. And since he's a computer genius none of us can crack the code.

Eighteen

The reference library is full of silence, but it's not the scary kind – it's friendly and peaceful, people reading and writing and minding their own business. No one takes any notice of me. The librarian has fetched me the books I want which Mr Merchant told us about, and I start to read about the cholera that hit this city in July 1832, after it had crept through the county on its nasty, germy feet. Here goes. Dad'll be pleased with me.

Where the rich lived was clean, pleasant and leafy. But in the other parts the narrow, winding streets were full of rubbish, sewage and animals scavenging for food. People kept pigs under the old city walls. Everything was thrown out on to the streets or into the river. Any old muck. Then they drew water out of the same river for drinking and washing. Often a dozen houses shared one lavatory. (My mind boggles – oh, no, not bog-less.)

Some water came from *our* Well and the underground passages where Sir had taken us, but people had to take their turn in long queues for just a pitcher of water from the slow-flowing river.

When news of the cholera came to the city, the Board of Health ordered the red flannel belts. These were useless and a waste of money. Water carts tried to clean the streets, but many more were needed. Streets were whitewashed. Made no difference, the cholera raged on.

The smell was horrific – dirt, sewage, animals and death. Tar was burnt to disguise it, but that smelt awful too. All bedding and clothes had to be burnt – which meant more grief and misery for the poor, who didn't have much in the way of bedding and clothes to begin with.

People died quickly: alive in the morning, dead at night. The numbers of the dead rose higher and higher throughout the summer months of 1832. It was hard to keep up with the burials.

It's like the terrible pictures of global disasters, I thought, the dreadfulness that follows floods, fires, volcanoes – it was like that that year, all around our school. The 'pester house' (the old plague house) was full. They turned our school into a hospital. (This is it. I'm getting there, I think.)

People were scared stiff. The cholera brought more

horrors. People lay dead in the street before being carted away. Wild things happened, bad things, drunkenness and cruelty and terrible mistakes – but there was kindness and consideration too. People looked after one another, cared for each other, comforted each other, especially the poor.

But – and it's a big BUT – here the description of things that happened is GHASTLY. (NB. Ghastly – ghostly?) I can't stop reading . . . HORROR! And then I read:

But the most lamentable and unnatural instance of neglect which happened was that of some children by their father: this man, having bedding and ample accommodation, placed his two dying children (H. and S.L., 22 Aug.) on the landing of the staircase upon straw, and there they both died; his sole reason for this inhumanity being the saving of his goods.

Oh, no. Oh, no, no, no, no!

Cass's nudging me.

'You finished? It's time to go. Come on.'

We creep out.

'Find out what you want?' she asks.

'Yeah. I think . . . I think I have.'

It's a bit hairy at home. In fact it sucks, right now. Teggy's back and we're all lined up in front of Mum and Dad. Romilly, Mizza, Cass, Cameron, Kris, me and Tegs. Mum has her 'hanging judge' look, very stern, and Dad tries to look as if he's serious and strict as well.

Here we go:

Videos to be checked by a parent before use.
Early bed for all. ('Even me?' shrieks Romilly.)
Homework and music practice table on wall to be ticked off.
Exercise Programme for all plus Healthy Eating Programme.
NO MORE GRANDAD *except for visits to his and Grandma's grave with a parent.*
No more Point Horror, Goosebumps *or any other horror stories or magazines.*
No piercing except for ears.
No clubbing. (Romilly, Cameron, Mizza all shriek.)
No cigarettes, no alcohol, no illegal substances ANYONE.

'She's not a lawyer – she's a prison warder,' mutters Mizza.

Then Mum and Dad go out of the room and hell breaks loose. Nobody, nobody is going to abide by those rules.

'If they want trouble, they can have it,' hisses Cameron, pulling up his shirt to show both nipples with really groovy studs in them.

'I'll have my tongue done tomorrow!' shouts Mizza, bouncing up and down in fury.

'I'm off out . . . ' Romilly says. 'My new boyfriend won't stand for all that Christopher Robin crap! Cass, where are you off to?'

'To do my practice,' Cass says calmly. 'And I'd wait a bit before you all start rebelling. It'll calm down, you see. They won't be able to keep it up.'

'And it's Teggy's fault,' Mizza swings round on her. 'You started this lot – you and your precious Grandad!'

Teggy thins her mouth, slits her eyes, then kicks Mizza hard on the shin. She's very powerful, built like a tank, is Tegs, whereas Mizza's just a Thin Lizzy.

As Mizza howls in pain and hops up and down, Tegs grabs my hand and we escape right up to my room in the attic and bolt the door – then fling ourselves on the bed. I'm bushed.

At last I say, 'These ghosts of yours. Are they two children, Tegs?'

'Yeah, course. They got shut out of their house by their dad when they got cholera. That's why there's all the doors that won't open. And they died unhappily. Later, their bodies were brought to school, or they tried to get in there and died, because the plague was so bad. Then it was a sort of hospital. I think they were somewhere near the staffroom. That's what Grandad says, anyway. It makes sense.'

(What sort of sense? Mad crazy sense?)

'But aren't you scared?'

'No, what's to be scared of? I'm Teggy. They're them.'

'But you must tell Mrs Markham. It fits what I read in the cholera book in the library. Or tell somebody. Some people.'

'I do. All the time. They don't listen.'

'No. Shall I tell them?'

'They won't listen to you either.'

'But we've got to help them and stop the happenings.'

'Grandad'll tell me when it's time.'

'Tegs – your name should be Cass, short for Cassandra.'

'But I'm Tegwyn Maddy Watson. Cass is Cassandra. Who was she anyway?'

'She told people what would happen.'

'And what did happen?'

'All sorts. But nobody believed her, either.'

'Don't worry, Snaggle. I've got chewing gum in my pocket. Have a bit. It's a bit old, OK?'

So we lie on the bed and chew, and at last I fall asleep.

Nineteen

Home's grim so I'm glad to be back at school. I want to see Shahid and Strawberry and talk about the *Chronicle* again. They've been ill, too. So's half the school. The mystery illness nearly closed it. But at least it wasn't cholera. And speaking of cholera, I want to talk to Sir about it. I'm looking for him when what I find – round the corner, pushed against a wall – is Boris, almost crying. Again.

The Girl Gang is there too, but watching this time. And Matthew Ernest and Rod Stringer. Watching, not doing anything, while kids from the other class in our year shove round Boris – waiting for one of them to begin what they've all got in mind.

'He started it. We didn't have ghosts and plagues here before. It all came with him. Why should we have him here in our school? We don't have to have HIM here!' said Barry Morse, a troublemaker and the ringleader.

'He doesn't belong 'ere!'

'OUT! OUT! OUT!'

'He's filthy. Get 'im out!'

'Fleas bring disease and Boris has fleas!'

'OUT! OUT! OUT!'

'Stop it!' I yell. 'Boris, I'm here. Boris!'

He looks up. He's not crying. But he is *sooo* scared. Poor Boris. He's full of fear. I can feel it. His fear.

'I'll get a teacher, Boris. Hang on!'

Strawberry runs up beside me.

'You horrible lot,' she screams. 'Leave him alone. He's done nothing to you!'

'What's it to you? Get lost or you'll get it, too!'

Shahid joins me and Strawberry, but more kids make a ring round us so we can't break out.

'Nosy-Parker, Snaggle-Waggle, Bossy-Wossy,' voices shriek.

'Lucy!' yells Strawberry. 'Fetch Sir!'

'OUT! OUT! OUT!'

The first stone hits Boris. Tears stream down his face.

This can't be happening. Not here.

'Stop it!' I'm shouting.

'You can't! Go and write it in your Chronic-rubbish nobody reads . . . '

'Sally . . . Sally – get Sir.'

'I daren't,' cries Sally. 'They won't let me.'

Half the school's here. Have they gone mad?

And round the corner strolls Ryan, idly swinging the baseball bat that's in his hand. He doesn't say anything. Never did say much, Ryan.

The noise drops. Everyone's watching him. After a minute, he calls: 'Snaggle, Shahid, Strawberry . . . '

Kids in the ring drop arms to let us through.

'Sally – fetch Sir. Eh?'

Someone yells, 'OUT! OUT! . . . '

Ryan swings the bat, then points it towards him, and he stops just as Sally shoots away and the Girl Gang starts up:

> Ryan's the greatest,
> Ryan's King,
> Ryan's the latest,
> Come on. Sing!

But Barry Morse isn't giving up the fun so easily.

'I'm still getting you, gyppo!' and picks up another stone. Ryan shoves out his left foot, tripping him up, and Boris runs towards us just as . . .

'I knew it! Causing trouble AGAIN! The minute I saw this mob I knew you would be in the middle of it, you wicked boy. I'll get you this time, Tiler. You'll be *excluded*, all right. And I'll send a report to your next school. It's my duty to let them know what they're getting. Come on, all of you. Run away and play. Don't let Ryan Tiler lead you into bad behaviour. At this school we'll keep up standards of excellence!'

Mrs Somers has, of course, arrived.

'But it wasn't Ryan,' I begin, 'who . . . '

'Be quiet. You've always got too much to say for yourself. Like that mother of yours. She's always had a big idea of herself and too much to say . . . '

I open my mouth, then close it again. What's the use? She'll never listen. And Sir is running here with Sally. And he will. And he does.

Twenty

Next day all the top year is brought into the hall, where Mrs Markham talks to us about bullying. Everyone stands silent and meek, trying to look as if they never did anything wrong, ever. I've tried to talk to Sir, but he's busy working out who actually started the row, and when I do catch him he's rushing off to a meeting and says he'll see me later. But he doesn't, of course – oh, no. He goes down with the mystery illness that isn't cholera and stays at home.

I don't feel like talking to anyone else because . . . because when I'm not with Teggy it all sounds like rubbish. What is there after all?

Two raggedy figures – possibly seen when a car is trashed.
Doors that won't open.
Me being scared – in the teachers' loo and after school. That could be just my imagination.
The cholera account in the reference library.

Missing SATs papers.
Mystery illness – which everyone says is caused by a virus.
Grandad, Teggy and Boris's Gran prophesying. They're mad
anyway.

Not much, is it? Can't go to Mrs Markham with *that*. She's like Mum – 'Get on with your work and don't worry. Have an early night and get plenty of sleep.'

I start to say all this to Shahid and Ryan and Strawberry.

'It's imagination and coincidence,' shrugs Shahid, looking clever and snooty.

'Crap,' says Ryan and walks off for a cricket practice.

That leaves Strawberry. 'You're right, of course,' she says. 'I think the school's haunted.' But she always agrees with nearly everybody, to keep them happy.

'But Teggy says it's always been haunted. So what's the difference now?'

'I dunno.'

(Neither do I, I say to myself. Forget it, Snaggle. Cricklepit Fair Day is on the way.)

Sir and nearly everyone else returns to school. And it's Cricklepit Fair and Pageant time. When half the school went down with the mystery virus it was nearly cancelled, but now we are all getting ready for Saturday, the great Cricklepit Fair day.

It's an all-day do, starting at ten in the morning and going on till ten at night. Bands and singers from far and wide, craft stalls, paint workshops, face painting, a bouncy castle, puppet making, greasy poles, story-telling, coordinated chaos, burger stalls, sweet stalls, ice cream, jewellery, knitwear, archery, white elephant, fortune telling (*a-a-a-r-g-h!*), ten bands (including Cricklepit's own), Japanese drums, South American samba, indie, rock and punk, African sing-alongs, refreshments and a bar – and to finish, an all-in disco to dance the night away.

In the middle of all this, at three o'clock, the celebra-tions will pause, and we'll perform our pageant – *Cricklepit Thro' the Ages*. This means walking through the streets, the playground, the school and all the stalls, games, and bands, and ending up in the school hall led by Lucy Chinn as St Sativola. The procession also includes Ryan, Shahid, Matthew, Rod and Boris as Saxons and Vikings. Shahid's wearing white make-up and a blonde wig, and he's left off his specs so he can't see much. Teggy and Mariella are little Victorian maidens (rich and healthy – not poor and dying of cholera) scattering rose petals. And nearly every-body's something – except for me. They got me to write the pageant play, so I'm hidden with the script as it gets going on the hall stage, with the school flautists and violinists playing the music. All the other activities take a break here, and lots of people come into the hall to watch the story of St Sativola, dated from about AD 740.

I didn't much want to write this pageant, as Lucy Chinn was going to be the Saint, but they said I didn't have to be in it if I wrote it – so I had a bash. It was the story I read in the underground passages. St Sativola is very good and kind to the poor – what about poor Boris, I think – and she and her Dad and Mum are jolly happy till Mum kicks the bucket (sorry – dies) and the wicked stepmother arrives.

She takes an instant dislike to Sativola and treats her harshly, especially when she finds out that she will inherit all her father's land. So she plots with some wicked servants, bribing them with gold to murder Sativola.

The servants are reaping in a field by the Well when Sativola comes to draw water. She offers them some, but they kill her and cut off her head with a scythe and then flee. Her brother finds her headless body later. (This was quite hard to stage – but Penny Farthing's very clever.)

Later she is recognised as a saint and the church is named after her. (Query: is this *Chronicle* material? Doubt it.)

And still she haunts our school, according to Teggy, Sally Fox and various other people.

I peep through the curtains while the play is going on, and I can see Mrs Somers wearing a huge hat with flowers on it and a long floaty dress all hung about with jewels, next to Mrs Markham in jeans and a T-shirt with 'Cricklepit School' printed on it. The Mayor's there and the vicar and Mum and Dad, oh and everyone! But not Romilly and co. – they're at their own schools.

The play's nearly over, and they're getting ready to do their *Thro' the Ages* parade again – and I'm taking a break, 'cos it wasn't too ghastly even if it had got the Chinny Wonder in it, and I look through the window behind the curtains. It's getting very dark – maybe a thunderstorm with an enormous grey cloud hovering over Cricklepit School, but you can see the car park, and there's Rod, dressed as a Viking, fiddling with the door of a new silver Beetle. What's he up to? He's supposed to be with us. And I know his brother's got a new car, but I'm sure it's not a Beetle. Large drops of rain begin to fall, and I watch him move away and slip in through the stage door at the back, when I'm called:

'Author! Author! Come and take a bow.'

So I go forward and bow, feeling like a prat, and I hear Mrs Markham say, 'I hope it doesn't rain on us all . . .'

'Oh, no,' exclaims Mrs Somers loudly, 'the sun always shines on OUR school.'

At that moment an enormous sword of lightning splits the sky and black clouds rush together, blotting out the sun, blue skies, the lot, and down falls the rain. And it's not just ordinary rain, it's a torrent, a cascade, a flood, steel rods of rain, a deluge, crashing thunder and laser lightning battling overhead. It's terrifying and people are screaming.

Boris's grandmother suddenly appears at the doorway, a black figure in a black cloak, her black eyes gleaming . . .

> *Until the cruelty stops*
> *Until the end of pain*
> *Doors will not open*
> *Waters will rise again!*

she cries, then she lifts up her arms – just as well she's not holding the peg basket this time – and points her finger at the school. Then she turns and glides away over the water.

'We're all going to die!' screams Sally Fox.

Twenty-One

The new Head Teacher, Mrs Markham, stands on a table on the hall platform, shouting instructions into a megaphone through the open doors to all corners of the school, which looks as if it's going to sink like the *Titanic* under the weight of water pouring down from the roof, flowing in through the windows, spouting up through the drains. The playground's a river rushing over the asphalt, swirling round the trees and the cars in the car park, to the field and the stalls and the games, the bouncy castle and all the gear for the Cricklepit Fair, on its way through the town down to the river and out to sea . . . In the middle of the chaos is Violet the caretaker, legs wide apart, hair purple as the thunderclouds rolling above the school explode out into thunder and jagged lightning, so the noise and the weird lights are nightmare country – Strobe-land. She's working like ten people, sweeping the water out of the school doors. Her huge husband, Cyril, has come in from their house next door and stands miles higher than anyone else, lifting furniture and books and little ones out of danger. Strawberry's comforting them.

And the hall is crowded with kids all dressed up for the pageant and their parents and teachers, laughing, yelling, splashing, crying. Wham! Sploosh! Swoosh! The storm came so fast out of nowhere that no one had time to get ready for it. Bands and stallholders and teachers are frantically hauling equipment to safety.

'Get a boat,' somebody yells.

'Yeah, a lifeboat,' Ryan shouts. 'That's what we need!'

Mrs Somers, the Chair of Governors, splashes like a great walrus towards us, holding on to her hat. She can hardly move in her drenched long dress.

'Put your backs into it, you children!' she yells.

'We'll drown if we do that!' Ryan shouts, towering over her.

'Oh, it's *you*, is it?'

'Yes, it's me. But I didn't start this lot. You can't blame me *this* time.'

She turns away. Ryan pretends to shove her down into the water, but stops and splashes me instead, so I'm wringing wet, sopping, saturated, soaked. But then we all are – a school for sponges. I try to push *him* down into the water, but he's too strong for me and I end up flat in the flood, shrieking as all the props of the pageant, and books, folders, posters and tapes float all around me – a year's work heading out ... where? Down the drain? Out to sea?

'This horrible year!' calls out Mr Merchant to Mrs Markham.

'All this damage, the awful waste,' she splutters. I think she's crying, but Head Teachers don't cry, do they? And it's hard to tell, as a torrent of extra-high water surges past us, on and on through our school, carrying shields, helmets, cloaks and swords.

'Everything's drowning!' cries Matthew. 'It's the end of Cricklepit School!'

A stomach-grabbing scream splits the air. Mrs Somers slips, and a table crashes on her with all the chairs piled on it. She's pinned down in the water under the chairs. Mr Merchant and Violet struggle towards her as she tries to free herself, but she's hurt. Her hat's fallen off and her yellow curls go drenched and stringy in the water, and she looks not like Mrs Somers, JP, Chair of Governors, Terror of Cricklepit School – but like a feeble old woman in need of care and assistance.

And it arrives. Getting there before the others, Ryan is at her side. He pushes off the chairs and table and lifts her up as Sir splashes over to them with Violet. Many hands carry her to safety on the platform.

As I try to reach them, heavy trainers and sopping

gear dragging me down, though at least I'm not in Saxon garments, I hear Ryan saying, 'You'll be all right, Mrs Somers. I'll look after you.'

So that's why Strawberry says he's a saint, I'm thinking, when I hear him whispering, 'This hurts you more than it hurts me.' There's a bit of a grin on his wet face.

Here we are on the stage, together with the rising flood waters.

'Huh,' mutters Ryan, 'that's great. We're all gonna drown and I still haven't found out who trashed the car.'

'The ghosts, maybe?'

'Oh, don't talk stupid, Snaggle. That's crap!'

Watching Rod splash up to us, a flashback shoots into my mind – Rod in the car park, fiddling with the silver Beetle. And I know.

'You, it was you! You trashed the car. You did it, Rod. I know it was you!'

He turns and starts to slosh away, but he's gone red. He shouts over his shoulder, 'Don't talk rubbish! You ain't blaming me for what I didn't do.'

He looks terrified as Ryan moves towards him, full of menace. Ryan's just about the scariest kid I know.

'I bet it was you. You're mad about cars. You're always going on about them,' he spits.

Thunder crashes above us, simultaneously with the

streak of lightning. The storm's right above us now. Rod tries to move more quickly, but he stands no chance. Ryan grabs him and plunges him face down into the water. Rod's head emerges, spluttering.

'Going to tell the truth now?'

'I didn't do it! I swear!'

Ryan pushes his head down again. I grab his arm to stop him. Ryan scares me stiff in this mood. He shrugs me off.

'Tell the truth!'

Rod comes up, streaming, terrified, stuttering, 'I didn't mean it. I never meant it. I didn't want to wreck the bloomin' car. Don't duck me again! Please, Ryan, let me go.'

'Tell me, then.'

'Nobody was around and I wanted – I wanted to drive it. It was all brand new and shiny. My Dad's broken into cars. I seen him do it, but I didn't mean to, Ryan, honest. I wuz just gonna drive it around a bit and put it back. But the wall got in the way. I didn't mean it. It wuzn't really, Ryan, honest, it wuzn't really my fault . . . '

Beside us, Mrs Somers tries to sit up.

'Well, why did you say it was ME who did it, then?' roars Ryan, seizing him again and holding him underwater, longer this time. Bubbles come to the surface. Rod struggles uselessly.

'Watch out! Don't drown him! Stop it, you idiot. Stop it, Ryan!'

Somehow the doors have jammed and WON'T OPEN. And still the water pours in. People are battering at the doors and climbing up the wall bars to try and open the windows, but the hall is shut tight. Everyone's yelling, giving orders. Panic's setting in. Above the din Ryan is shouting, 'I'm gonna kill him! Vandal! Sneak!' and hitting Rod.

'Stop,' croaks Mrs Somers. 'It wasn't him who told me.'

Ryan releases Rod. He crawls back to the stage, gasping.

'I never said it was you, Ryan. I nick cars, but I'm not a grass. I don't tell tales. I don't know who said it was you.'

'Who was it, then?'

Mrs Somers raises her head.

'Matthew Ernest told me it was you, Ryan,' she says.

Matthew's moving away, pushing through the water as quickly as possible. He'll swim for it if he has to, through the rapidly rising waters.

(Bits of me that aren't scared stiff think what a brilliant article this will make. But they'll never let me print it.)

'And you believed him?' Ryan's roaring like a bull, shaking his fist, his face bright red. 'Matthew, you creep, why did you? What did I ever do to you?' Despair and misery are stamped all over Ryan.

Rain splats down on us. The roof will come down soon.

Matthew's talking now, words rattling like popcorn being heated up.

'Yes, it was me, 'cos I hate you, Ryan Tiler. You're a big-head. You think you're so great at everything. All the girls fancy you. Ryan this, Ryan that, the Ryan Fan Club. I was really cheesed off when they let you come back. I wanted you excluded for ever. Give others a chance. Like me. I tried and tried and I didn't get in the first team. My Dad was gutted. He was in it when he was a kid here. And I know I've mucked up the SATs and Mum will be mad. But you, you – you even went out with Lucy. I wanted to. You did, and you dumped her and she still didn't like *me*. NO ONE DOES!!!'

'Oh, poor Matthew,' someone says. It can only be Strawberry. He turns to her and his tears fall into the water along with the rain.

Ryan staggers and holds on to the platform, looking shattered.

'Don't hit me,' sobs Matthew. 'Don't hurt me, Ryan.'

'What's the point of hurting you, you miserable scrawny little runt?' Ryan shouts. 'Oh, what the heck!' He's nearly crying, too!

'But why didn't you say who it was?' he asks Mrs Somers.

'How could I? His mother's my best friend. Matthew's my godson, you see . . . '

And out of the watery chaos and the rising mist comes Teggy, with Mariella and Boris in tow. Teggy climbs on the table with Mrs Markham. Still the rain hammers down. Something's happening, it's changing. But the mist's thicker and I can't see very well, and I'm deafened by the loudest thunderclap ever. I can't think. Where's Dad? Where's Sir? Where's Mum? The waters rise and rise. Where's it all coming from? What's gonna happen to us?

Teggy is pointing at someone. Lucy Chinn. What the heck is she pointing at her for? At least I think it's Lucy, but she's wearing her pageant outfit as the Saint – yuck – so it's hard to tell, what with the roar of the water, the shouts, the mist. I can see Mrs Somers holding Ryan's hand. She seems to be saying sorry, but I'm probably just going crazy.

Still pointing at the Chinn, Teggy yells, 'Stop it!'

'I wish I could,' cries Mrs Markham.

'How? Tell me how?' yells Sir.

'Not you! St Thingy!' shouts Teggy.

She waves all round at the dripping roof, the flooding floor, then back to Lucy Chinn, who's grown long fair plaits, and stands about six feet tall in a shimmering robe. The mist round her head is turning gold, as if the sun's shining through it.

'Tell them to stop it NOW! There's no need any more. They're found. They're safe.'

And there's silence.

Teggy turns to me. 'It's over, Snaggle. They'll go now, the children. It's all over.'

In the silence, the school bell once rung by Ryan Tiler's cousin rings out loud and clear.

Outside sirens wail. Doors are flung open. Water washes away down the field and playground. I hold out my hands. No rain drops on them. It's stopped.

Fire engines, ambulances, police, firemen – everyone from everywhere, it seems – helping people to safety. Mrs Somers lets go of Ryan's hand as she's carried away on a stretcher.

It's over, whatever it was – flash flood, cloudburst, Cricklepit School's own storm – all gone, finished. And, oh, I'm *sooo* knackered and soaked.

But Violet's husband Cyril shouts down, from where he's lifting a kid from a very high cupboard. 'I've found them. They were here all the time. I remember now. I put them up here to be safe when we were having that special clean-up after the office door kept sticking. They're safe, Vi. High and dry, in a polythene folder. It's THEM SATS!'

Sir's talking to Lucy Chinn, who looks her ordinary yuck self, only more so, being very wet.

'You all right? You looked a bit strange, just now.'

'I felt strange. I'm OK now, but I felt peculiar, as if I wasn't here. As if I was someone else. It was that Teggy Watson pointing at me. I never did like her. And I don't feel very well. I want Mummy. Where's she got to? Mummy, Mummy!'

'Lucy, Lucy, Lucy, my darling baby. I'm here. You're all right now. What did they do to you? Come to Mummy, Lucy.'

Our mother is also embracing Teggy and me, which she doesn't do very often, and I find it embarrassing. But Teggy clings to her and sobs.

'What's the matter? Seems to me like you sorted it out, Tegs.'

'Grandad's gone. Went with the children. Said he'd done what he'd got to do, something about being a governor and he was knackered so he was off and . . . I shall miss him, wah, wah, wah!'

For once my mother doesn't say a thing, just hugs her tight.

'Mrs Markham, ma'am,' the Chief Fireman says.

'Yes?'

'Two small skeletons have been washed up in the gully and drain under the old staffroom. We'd like you to come and look at them.'

THE LAST CRICKLEPIT CHRONICLE

THE EYES – THE EARS – THE VOICE – OF THE SCHOOL

Editor	*Assistant Editor*	*Reporter*
Snaggletooth Watson	Shahid Malik	Strawberry Rainbird

Special Edition

So this is it, folks! The *last Chronicle* — hope you enjoyed reading it.

Clearing up after the Flood. Mr Merchant has asked for volunteers to help in the school holiday under the leadership of Mrs Jefferson-Smythe.

A short service was held for the burial of the children's skeletons discovered in the recent flood. At school a memorial plaque will be mounted on the wall near where they were found.

The school bell has been mended and it is to be re-hung and the school roof mended!

AWARDS

Shahid Malik — Maths

Snaggle Watson — Computer Studies

Strawberry Rainbird — English

Lucy Chinn — Dance

Tasha Santini — Music

Santia Bliss — Languages

Boris Ladislaw — Greatest Progress in Maths and Literacy

Ryan Tiler — Games and Athletics. Ryan is to be congratulated on obtaining a place at a famous football academy.

We wish all who are leaving the best of luck in their new schools.

GOSSIP

Mrs Somers JP has resigned as Governor. Her place is to be taken by Mr B. Watson.

Mr Merchant's book *An Account of the Cholera Epidemic of 1832* is to be published by Sackcloth and Ashes on September 9th.

Mr Armstrong, PE teacher and Miss P. Farthing are to be married on August 20th. We wish them tons of happiness. Anyone who turns up is welcome, says Penny.

A stray black cat has taken up residence in the school and is to be called Lucky. It is already dealing with the mice which Gowie Corby, a former pupil, introduced into the school.

Mr Steve Stringer (Rod's father) has won £1.5 million on the lottery and the family is moving to a new town (name not known). So far he's bought a Ferrari, a Porsche and an Aston Martin for starters. Goodbye, then, Rod. And it's also goodbye to Boris and Matthew.

End-of-Term Disco

A fantastic time was had by all. Dates, dumping and weeping from all leavers.

This is the Last Chronicle

We tried to bring you the news
We tried to tell you the truth.
It's up to you, kids, to decide if the school was haunted.

Goodbye from:
Snaggletooth Watson
Strawberry Rainbird
Shahid Malik